Licked

BROOKE BLAINE

Copyright © 2015 by Brooke Blaine
www.brookeblaine.com
Edited by Arran McNicol
Cover by Hang Le
Formatted by Ella Frank

No part of this book may be reproduced or transmitted in any form or by any means, electronic or mechanical, including photocopying, recording, or by any information storage and retrieval system without the written permission of the author, except for the use of brief quotations in a book review.

This book is a work of fiction. Names, characters, places, and incidents either are products of the author's imagination or are used fictitiously. Any resemblance to actual persons, living or dead, events, or locales is entirely coincidental.

Also by Brooke Blaine

L.A. Liaisons Series

Licked (Book One)

Hooker (Book Two)

Romantic Suspense

Flash Point

Co-authored with Ella Frank

Sex Addict

To my Susie Q—

You would've gotten this story a lot sooner if you hadn't read my diary to your friends all those years ago.

Chapter One
Reunion with a Sex God

THE HIGH SCHOOL gymnasium smelled like freshly waxed floors, Polo Sport, and bad decisions. As I peered up at the gaudy blue and gold banner hanging precariously across the open double doors that proclaimed, "Welcome Back, Warriors," a roll of nausea filled my gut.

A few small steps through that entrance would send me hurtling back into my past. *Ten years* back into my past, to be precise.

Speaking of bad decisions, this was up there on the list of all-time stupidest things I've done in my life. Why had I thought coming back here was a good idea? It wasn't like I even enjoyed high school, what with the popular girls the size of my thigh, the strange meatloaf they served every day that could be classified as a mystery food, and the never-ending ridicule I'd faced after being caught stuffing my bra during gym class.

What? Those swing dresses weren't gonna fill themselves.

Truth be told, I came here for one reason, and one reason only: I wanted to show Cameron Mathis I was finally a woman worth noticing.

I know what you're thinking. Who's Cameron Mathis and yeah, he's got a dreamy name, but why the hell should I care?

Just wait. Wait for it…

Where was I? Oh yes. So, now here I was, the product of ridiculous fantasies regarding that certain someone and peer pressure from my best friends, all of whom had never set foot into Woodland High and couldn't believe there'd ever been an awkward Ryleigh Phillips at any age.

But alas. There was. And it was a glaring reminder, now that I was here, that me and my black and white strapless rockabilly dress didn't belong. My past was making me claustrophobic, the pale green walls that hadn't changed in the last decade closing in.

Fingering the beaded necklace that sat just above my collarbone, I slowly backed away from the doors, the click-clack of my cherry heels against the vinyl tile moving in time to the band playing inside.

I hadn't been seen yet, so I could sneak out of here and no one would be the wiser. *Yes. Brilliant idea.* Kicking off my shoes and relaxing with a huge bowl of ice cream sounded like a perfect—

The roar of male voices echoing up the hall to my right knocked me out of my sugar daydream, and I froze momentarily before whipping around and searching for a quick exit. There was only one, at the very end of the hall, and I made a mad dash before there were witnesses to my appearance here.

And then it happened. The moment that would change my life forever.

Just as I crossed the intersection, a tall, muscular body rounded the corner and smacked into me, causing me to lose my balance and reach out for something to grab on to. And that something, my friends, was Cameron Mathis's penis.

Yes, *that* Cameron Mathis. Completely gorgeous former football God and sole object of my high school fantasies. The one I'd braved the nightmare of Reunionville for. *And now, the owner of the bare cock in my hand.*

Wait—bare?

My eyes went wide as I looked down to his pelvis and stared, unbelieving, at the hot flesh of manstick in my hands.

"Oh my God," I whispered.

"Ryleigh Phillips." The rich baritone of his voice had me looking up at the face it belonged to. Cameron's sea-blue eyes held mine as one side of his mouth turned up in amusement.

How do you know my name? I wanted to ask, but then I remembered I was not that meek teenager with a schoolgirl crush anymore. *No way. I'm a poised, assertive woman with a thriving business who never has a problem finding a date. Well, when I have time for one. Which lately has been…oh, never.*

"That would be me," I said, my hand still gripping him like a vise. Though it seemed to be hardening underneath my fin—

"Cameron," he said.

I blinked. "What?"

He laughed, a sexy, throaty sound. "You look like you don't remember me. Cameron Mathis. We were in the same Spanish class all four years."

Holy Jesus, how did he know that? And then a random thought: *Why don't I remember more from those classes than how to count to twenty?*

But as I took in the perfectly gelled, sun-kissed blond hair and the brilliant white smile that was nearly blinding, I realized exactly why I'd never paid attention in class. Who could concentrate when they had a living Ken doll to fantasize about for hours on end?

"Right…right," I said, my mind buzzing. He had to be joking if he thought anyone in this town didn't know who he was. Students and teachers alike had bowed down to the guy after he'd taken them to the state championships four years running.

When his gaze dropped between us to the hold I still had on him, I flushed and quickly let go.

"Oh, God. Sorry. Uh…I don't normally grab, um…other appendages instead of hands to shake."

A rumbling laugh came from his chest. "Well, that's a shame. It's a nice way to say hello."

My cheeks flamed hotter, and I could only shake my head. Before I could utter another apology, the booming voices I'd heard moments earlier came running down the hallway past us, every one of the guys naked as the day they were born—except for their shoes.

"What the hell…" I said, more to myself than Cameron, as I watched them run by. Shrieks of laughter from inside the building rang out, and I raised an eyebrow at the naked man in front of me.

"Sorry about the run-in," he said with a wink, his smile sexy and full of confidence as he backed into the gymnasium to join them. "You know how dares go. I'll come find you when I have some clothes on." And then he turned and jogged into the room, the spectacular muscles of his ass flexing with each step.

Did that just happen? Holy…mother.

I was vaguely aware of my phone when it started to ring, and it took me a few seconds to shake off the daze before I answered.

"Ryleigh? Do I have to tell you there's an emergency and you need to come back to the shop right now to have shots with us?" one of my fabulous foursome BFFs, Shayne, asked over the line.

"You're not even in town right now to have shots

with if I said yes. Aren't you supposed to be at a wedding? Or do you need me to save you from that too?"

Shayne gave a dramatic sigh. "Bloody hell, it's a nightmare. The groom caught the bride shagging his brother before the ceremony, and he's been chasing him around the car park for half an hour already. Paige ducked over to the reception bar to get us drinks." Shayne's Australian accent was out in full force, as it tended to do when she was excited or pissed. Well, not *pissed* in the drunk sense like she'd say, though I had no doubt with Paige there they'd be that too in a matter of minutes.

"Tell her not to forget the popcorn for the show."

"I'm sure they'll be passing that out any minute. So. Did you run into Cameron yet?"

Oh, did I ever. With a wry smile, I said, "You could say that."

"And?"

"And I think I'm gonna stick around for a while."

"Fuck me. Go get him, Ry, and then call us after and tell us everything."

"I plan on it." I straightened the wide red belt at my waist and threw my shoulders back. "But Shayne? Don't wait up."

AN HOUR LATER, and my gamble had paid off. Cameron

had indeed found me after the group of former jocks decided to put their pressed suit pants and button-downs back on.

I know. Bummer, right?

And I swear I'm normally this cool, collected person, but seeing as this guy had been starring in my dirty dreams since I was fifteen, it was perfectly acceptable to be breaking a sweat. Especially if that happened to be on the dance floor.

It felt strange to be a part of his group, dancing among them like old friends. They had inside jokes and ridiculous signature dance moves—the "crack yo back" being my favorite—but somehow, when Cameron's attention was on me, it made me feel like the only person in the room.

Until his ex cut in.

"May I?" Lauren Gambel was a five-foot-two brunette powerhouse with a syrupy-sweet voice and a wardrobe fit for a Playboy Bunny. She also happened to be Cameron's high school sweetheart, though *sweetheart* wasn't something anyone outside of her glam squad of followers would ever attribute to her. To say she terrorized everyone back in the day would be like saying Attila the Hun was an unpleasant fellow. I doubted much had changed in ten years.

She stood there smiling at Cameron, her hand rubbing up and down his bicep in a familiar, territorial way. Then she cut her heavily lined eyes at me. "You don't mind if I steal him away, do you, Rebecca?"

"It's Ryleigh. And *I* mind," Cameron answered for me. His grip on my waist tightened as he pulled me closer, angling us so her hand slid off his arm. Moving us away, he called over his shoulder, "Go try Ted."

And oh, the daggers that denial got. It was all I could do not to laugh at the explosive look on Lauren's face. I did send her a friendly wave with the tips of my fingers, though, just before he spun me around.

I was—dare I say it—having *fun,* even with the death glares being sent my way. You would've thought Cameron and I were old friends reconnecting and not practically strangers who before tonight had never spoken a word to each other. Wait. That's not true. He did say thanks to me one time our junior year when a paper slid off his desk and I picked it up and handed it to him.

Oh my God, how pathetic that I even remember that.

I know—you don't have to say it. You're cringing on my behalf. Let me just slap myself and put my game face back on.

I am an amazing, independent woman who has impeccable taste and phenomenal friends. Not to mention I'm a mad genius who owns a thriving business and doesn't have to make up one that involves inventing Post-its.

There, much better.

"Drinks?" he asked when the song ended and the always lame Electric Slide took over.

"Please."

Grabbing my hand, he led the way through our

former classmates to the punch station. *Spiked* punch, I was positive. Cameron picked up two full cups, but when he saw Lauren sidle up next to him, he looked back at me and nodded at the exit door. I followed him out, not wanting to get caught up in another scene. Catfights were so not my thing.

The night air was warm, the breeze a soft caress on my skin, and I let out a happy sigh.

"Better?" he asked.

"Much." I took a sip of the punch and shuddered. Oh yeah. That bad boy was majorly spiked.

Cameron recoiled when he lifted the cup to his lips. "Holy shit, did they pour gasoline in here?"

"I was thinking it was formaldehyde."

"Yeah, we can do better than that," he said, tossing his cup into the trash bin. "Are you staying around here this weekend?"

"No, I don't live too far away. West Hollywood."

His brow rose. "You're kidding."

"Nope."

"I thought you'd be off in New York or something."

"Why would you think that?"

"Just…isn't that where people who like"—he pointed at my dress—"fashion-type stuff go?"

"I'm gonna take that as a compliment you think I could do something like that. Where are you these days?"

"Burbank."

What? "Burbank like…practically down the street?"

Stupid question, but I had to clarify.

His lips quirked up on one side. "Looks like we're neighbors."

No. No way. I had not been living mere miles from Cameron Mathis for years. My stomach flip-flopped. *Holy. Shit.*

Swallowing, I put back on confident Ryleigh. "You'll have to stop by my shop sometime. I'll even throw in a free—" I stopped when the sound of my favorite eighties ballad began to play. I must've gotten a little too excited, because a gasp escaped my lips as I looked toward the gym.

Cameron chuckled. "You like this song?"

"I love this song."

"Then we better not miss it." He took a step closer to me, and even in my heels I had to look up at him. His hand went around my waist, firm and pulling me closer. I swear I practically fell into his arms.

As we moved to the music, I was back at senior prom, but instead of that wallflower girl on the sidelines without a date, I had snagged the guy of my dreams. Had my hands not been gripping his muscled shoulders, I would've pinched myself.

"It's a shame we didn't hang out more," Cameron said, and he didn't have to finish his sentence for me to know the rest of what he meant. *Back then.* It was probably better that we hadn't; I wouldn't have been the recipient of his arms around me then.

He pushed a stray tendril of hair behind my ear, and

his eyes zoomed in on my mouth.

Oh hell. He had the look. The I'm-gonna-put-my-lips-on-yours-now-and-all-your-fantasies-will-come-true look.

He was going to kiss me. Right there. Steps away from our high school. In front of…okay, well, no one, but still. My eyelids fluttered shut, and my lips parted as his head inched closer…

"Caaaaaam," a slurred voice straight out of *Valley Girl* said before the owner draped herself over the side of Cameron's arm, pushing in between us so I stumbled out of his hold.

Lauren was back, but this time she'd definitely overdone it with the tequila perfume. Her red lipstick was starting to smear around the edges, and Cameron grabbed her shoulders and pushed her back before she could wipe herself off on his shirt.

"I was trying to find you," she told him, giving him a smile that I was sure she thought was flirty. *But no. Hot mess.*

Cameron held her upright as she swayed. "Maybe we should get you home. Or to your parents' house or wherever it is you're staying."

"Yes, good idea." Lauren giggled and pulled out a keycard, tapping it on her nose. "Maybe we should go to my hotel and—" She hiccupped, and her hand flew to her mouth like she was going to be sick. Her face turned a light shade of green, and…*here it comes.*

"That way," I said, pointing to low-lying bushes nearby. He hauled Lauren over to them just in time for her

Jose Cuervo dinner to come back up.

"Jesus, Lauren." Cameron shook his head as he backed away.

"You know…I seem to remember her in this position a lot in high school." I scrunched my nose. "I think it had more to do with getting rid of her lunch, though."

Cameron groaned and rubbed his forehead. "I'm so sorry about this."

I tried not to focus on the fact that our first kiss had been interrupted by a vomiting villainess. I supposed the bright side was that she didn't get sick *on* us, which would've taken the night to a whole different level.

Shrugging, I said, "It's not your fault. But are you sure you don't want to go with her? I mean, she does look pretty tempting."

"Hah, extremely. Too bad she's married."

My eyes went wide. "What?"

"Oh yeah. To the same guy she cheated on me with that knocked her up her first year of college." He looked me over, a curious expression on his face. "Didn't you stay in touch with anyone from here?"

Looking away, I struggled not to fidget under his gaze. How could I explain my lack of friends without sounding like a total loser? "Not really. A couple of girls, but they live on the East Coast now. I just…moved on."

"Moved on," he murmured, glancing back at Lauren, who was still heaving onto a poor succulent. "That's a good thing. You're better than this place."

I had no response for that. Not a "thank you," not a "but you don't know me," not a "damn right I am, thanks for noticing." Nada. It was all I could do to keep my jaw from dropping to the dirt.

The door to the gym pushed open, the muted sound of the music blasting like earplugs being yanked out.

"Lauren?" a high-pitched voice called out. One of the glam squad members searching for their queen. As the lithe figure stepped out onto the sidewalk, she called out her friend's name again but then stopped when she saw us. Her eyes narrowed as she looked me up and down before turning up her nose and focusing her attention on Cameron.

"The party's inside, you know," she told him.

"I know."

"Doesn't look like it."

"If you're looking for your friend"—he moved aside, revealing Lauren in the bushes just as she coughed—"maybe you could take her home?"

"Oh shit—Lauren?" Running over on wobbly heels, she reached for her friend's hair and held it off her face with one hand while pulling out her phone to text in the other. "Why didn't someone come get me? Why is she puking in the bushes and not in the bathroom? Where are your fucking manners, Mathis?"

She continued to babble as the rest of the squad began to file outside, her text obviously having sent a message to the masses. They flocked around Lauren in a protective circle while sending death glares our way.

Cameron sighed, loosening his tie as he moved toward me. "So."

"So."

He raised an eyebrow. "Wanna get out of here?"

Chapter Two

To Slut or Not to Slut...

I'D FOLLOWED CAMERON back to his place, which turned out to be a half-hour drive, traffic notwithstanding, from my apartment. *How the holy hell did Cameron Mathis live within breathing distance (okay, slight exaggeration), and I didn't know it?* I should've been able to feel him on some intrinsic level, surely.

Yeah, I know what you're thinking. Get a grip, Ryleigh. But I planned on getting a *very* good grip soon, spank you very much.

But first I needed some liquid courage. And wouldn't you know it, there just so happened to be a bar a couple blocks down from his place.

He held my hand as we walked to The Tavern. Sat across from me at a high-top table and actually paid attention to what I said for the who knows how many hours we sat there. He laughed at my jokes. Paid for our drinks and left a generous tip. Stood up when I went to the restroom—and never ever checked out another girl or even his cell phone.

That's it. We're getting married. No ifs, ands, or buts. The guy was perfect.

When we were ready to leave, he took my hand to help me down from the chair, and I caught his gaze drifting over my bare thighs, where my skirt had risen up to an indecent level. I let him continue looking before slowly smoothing it down. His eyes came up to mine, full of devilry, and he laced our fingers before walking us back to his place.

Cameron's house was nothing like what I expected. For a guy in his late twenties, he seemed to have his shit together. A rarity in L.A., where everyone pretended they were in their early twenties while pushing forty and still had the four roommates and movie-poster walls to prove it.

But Cameron had…green plants…like, living ones. And leather couches, a stainless steel kitchen, gorgeous lighting fixtures, and a… *What the hell?*

I crouched down next to the coffee table and touched my finger to the side of the glass as a blue fish swam up to meet it. "You have an aquarium for a coffee table," I said, shaking my head. Okay, so this must be the "bachelor" part of his pad. Even if Cameron hadn't been a six-foot-four Adonis, I'd bet this one talking piece alone would have women handing over their panties.

"You like it?" I heard Cameron ask from the kitchen.

I smiled as I ran my finger back and forth across the glass before going over to grab the much-needed bottle of water he offered. I took a long swallow before nodding.

"I do. It's absolutely—" As I turned my head to glance back at the aquarium table, my eyes caught sight of the enormous California king bed in the center of the room to my right, and I whispered, "Massive."

I couldn't seem to tear my gaze away as Cameron rounded the bar and came to stand in front of me. He set my water down and backed me against the counter.

If it was possible for hearts to beat so hard they flew out of your chest, mine would've. I felt the urge to pinch myself again, but Cameron's arms were on either side of my body, and I didn't dare move.

"I'm glad you decided to come," he said, his voice low and husky.

I was more than happy to come whenever he wanted. But… *Oh shit*. This was really happening. In minutes I would be on that bed…with Cameron…the insanely sexy man with his hands now on my—

"Um, do you mind if I have a minute?" I asked, pushing him back a little so I could look up at him. "Restroom?"

"I do mind," he said with a wink before nodding at an open door inside his bedroom. "It's right through there."

My fingers ran down his arms to where his hands

rested below my hips, and I gave a gentle squeeze. "Won't be long."

Before I shut the bathroom door behind me, I looked back to see Cameron follow me into the room and take a seat on the edge of the bed, his hands splayed out on either side of him, and his eyes hungrily tracking me.

And that look had me reaching for my phone and dialing one of the numbers on my short list of favorites. When Paige's voice came over the line, with what sounded like a party on full blast in the background, I said, "I need your help."

"Help? Hang on, let me go outside." The music faded and then she asked, "Where are you? Does Quinn need to come get you—"

"No," I whispered, moving to the far end of the bathroom and sitting on the edge of the tub. *Damn, he has a tub* and *a shower.* Maybe I needed to think about relocating. "I'm at Cameron Mathis's house."

"What?" she shrieked, and I could picture her eyes huge and gaping at me. "What the hell do you need help for, then? Go get him."

"I'm in his bathroom."

"Are you sick?"

"No."

"Are you showering together?"

"No."

"Then hang up the phone, Ryleigh, and get the fuck out of the bathroom."

See? When she put it like that, it sounded so easy.

My knee bounced up and down, both from impatience and also from being nervous as hell. "You have to tell me I should do this."

"I have to tell you to sleep with a gorgeous guy you've been crushing on since you were prepubescent? Really?" Paige tsked her disapproval. "I thought my promiscuous ways had rubbed off on you by now. You're breaking my heart."

"Well, it's just been…a while."

"Since wankjob Larry, right? Exactly why you should hop back in the saddle. I mean that quite literally."

"Oh God." I shook my head as I looked at the petrified reflection in the mirror. She didn't look anything like the confident woman that was usually there.

Why the hell was I freaking out? It wasn't like I was a virgin, and I'd dreamed about being the girl in Cameron Mathis's bed so many times that I'd gone through vibrator batteries like water.

So why the hesitation, Ryleigh? I was tempted to slap myself.

"Ry, do I need to read you the list?"

"Of course not—"

"Liar."

I sighed. "Okay, I think you might have to."

Paige cleared her throat, and in her most professional voice, the one that barked orders behind the scenes of hundreds of weddings while also showing a cool head for the bridal party, said, "Number one: You're good enough. You're smart enough. And doggonit, people like you."

With a groan, I shook my head. "Please not the Stuart Smalley affirmations, or I'm hanging up."

"Boo, you're no fun. Okay, number one: You can't die having let jizzface Larry be the last person you ever fucked. Number two: You're the owner of an enormously successful Ice Creamery & Booziery, which is getting ready to make its prime-time debut and possibly become a chain. This alone means you should be having sex to celebrate. And lots of it. Number three: I'm at a reception that not only is missing its bride and groom, but also ran out of alcohol an hour ago. Since I'm not drunk enough to sleep with any of these butterfaces, you have to take one for the team. Number four: You shaved tonight for a reason. Number five: Hello, you're fabulous. Gorgeous. And you have legs every woman would kill for and every guy would want wrapped around his waist."

"That last one is not on the list."

"Well, it's on the Paige list, and you did call me, so deal with it. Besides, it's true."

"You're so good for my ego."

"You're welcome. Please hang up the phone now and go tackle that hot piece of ass. I demand it."

"Going."

I hit the end button and bit my lip. I was about to have sex with Cameron Mathis. My inner seventeen-year-old was squealing and doing backflips across the damn high school gymnasium.

After triple-checking that I'd worn the sheer bikini panties instead of the spandex underwear I'd been tempted to sport to suck myself into this dress, I gave myself one last approving once-over.

No pressure, Ryleigh, but you're about to have the greatest night of your life.

But when I opened the door, that thought flew right the hell out of my head.

CAMERON MATHIS WAS passed out.

Like, fully passed out.

Like, fully passed out and still completely clothed.

Tiptoeing over to the bed, I poked him to make sure he wasn't just fucking with me, and a light snore came out.

Are you kidding me?

Crossing my arms, I stood over him and stared. He was flawless even in sleep, his face a kind of marbled beauty, like a prized possession you look at but don't touch.

And how true is that right now? There would be no touching tonight.

As much as part of me wanted his blue eyes to flick open and for him to pull me down on top of him, a strange relief washed over me to replace any disappointment.

With a sigh, I took his shoes off, careful not to wake him, and then pulled the covers down from the top of the bed. He was lying sideways, so I wrapped the blankets over him burrito style and tucked him in.

Well, hell. Do I stay, or do I go?

I'd had waaaay too much to drink tonight. So much so, I was starting to see two of him. If I called Quinn to pick me up, I'd never hear the end of it, plus I'd have to come back to get my car tomorrow. *Ugh. That option is out.* And if I were honest with myself, I wasn't ready to leave Cameron and never hear from him again, which would certainly happen if I left now.

With a yawn, I contemplated my sleeping arrangement options, eyeing the empty space on his bed. There was more than enough room for me, but…that was kind of weird, right? Getting in his bed when I wasn't technically invited there. *Yeah, no.*

I yawned again and went out to the living room. The couch did look comfy, and there was a blanket lying across the top of it. That was enough of a sign for me, and this way Cameron wouldn't think I'd tried to molest him in his sleep. Though the thought *was* a little tempting.

Kicking off my heels, I spread myself out on the soft leather and tossed the cover over my bare legs. Turning on my side, I watched the fish swimming around in the coffee table, looking for the pretty one I'd seen earlier. When a lumpy brown one swam past, all I could think was *Damn, that is one ugly fish.*

As if it'd heard me, it faced the glass. It looked like it'd gotten lip fillers or something. *Did fish even have lips?* Okay, maybe now I was super drunk. It stared at me, and I tried to stare back, but man, the thing was hideous. There was no way I could fall asleep with it watching me, so I flipped to my other side and pulled the covers up.

This not-sleeping-with-your-high-school-crush thing was for the best. There'd be no walks of shame, no awkward exchanges when we ran into each other at the twenty-year reunion. Yes, there was something to be said for keeping your skirt on.

But there was also something to be said for fantasies being hotter than real life, and it was with scandalous thoughts of what I *would've* done with Cameron that I drifted off to…

SOMEONE WAS WATCHING me.

I could feel their stare, feel a body looming over me. Maybe it was Cameron coming to kiss me awake, my very own prince come to life.

My eyelids fluttered open, a smile beginning to tip my lips as I looked up into—

Not Cameron's face.

"Oh my God," I said, yanking the covers up to my shoulders as a pair of eyes I'd never seen before watched me. They were dreamy eyes, like melted milk chocolate, and they would've been nice to fall into had they not been accompanied by a twinkle of amusement crinkling the edges.

"Mornin', sunshine." The gorgeous guy had a sexy voice to match, and it was then that I realized I must've still been dreaming.

Closing my eyes, I burrowed under the blanket and tried to fall back asleep, so that when I woke up again, I'd see the one I'd fallen asleep fantasizing about.

A deep laugh rumbled out above me. "I'm still here. Just thought you might want some coffee before Cameron's alarm goes off and he drinks it all."

I opened one eye. "Coffee?" I croaked.

He smiled at me then, his lips quirked up higher on one side, and my heart stuttered in my chest.

Holy hell. Who is he?

I couldn't seem to form coherent words, so when he asked, "Cream and sugar okay?" all I could do was nod, my brain not really taking in what he was saying. He could've been asking me if he could *dump* the cream and sugar on me and I would've agreed in that moment…as long as he promised to lick it off. *Wait, no. Bad Ryleigh.*

When he headed back toward the kitchen, I sat up, still clutching the blanket to my chest, and took the opportunity to get a good look at him.

The guy was tall, though not nearly as big as Cameron, and he wore a faded pair of jeans that had streaks of what looked like paint smeared in various spots across them. A simple black tee showed off his broad shoulders and tan arms, but before I could finish my perusal, he rounded the kitchen bar and was gone from my sight.

Then it occurred to me that I was probably hot-mess city. Pulling the compact out of my purse, I looked back to make sure he wasn't watching, and then took a peek at the damage.

I looked like the Creature from the Black Lagoon. Rubbing away the flakes of mascara from under my eyes, I cursed that I couldn't seem to wake up like they did in movies. You know, like an airbrushed model that doesn't have smeared lipstick, bedhead, and dried drool on the side of her cheek. When I noticed the open bathroom door near the kitchen, I grabbed my purse and heels and made a run for it.

What I saw in the mirror almost had me turning around and hightailing it out of the apartment. Holy fuck, that reflection was not gonna do.

I set about retouching my makeup—so grateful in this moment that I'm the girl who never leaves the house without her lipstick and powder—and reworked my hair into a messy ponytail. Then I brushed my teeth with my finger using the toothpaste sitting on the counter.

When I emerged, I felt not quite so horrendous. Which wasn't a remarkable step up from ratchet mess, but it would have to do for the moment.

Wait, why had I stayed here again? And why hadn't

it occurred to me that Cameron lived with someone? A really hot someone. *Damn.*

The stranger making me coffee raised an eyebrow when I came to a stop by the kitchen counter, almost as though he'd heard my thoughts, but more likely because I no longer looked like I'd been hit with an ugly stick.

"Hope you like it strong," he said as he pushed the steaming cup toward me.

Butterflies unleashed in my belly, and I didn't trust my legs to hold me up if I had to drink my coffee under his gaze, so I sat down on the barstool before picking the mug up and blowing into it.

"Thank you," I said.

Winking, he took a sip and swallowed. "Welcome."

The room fell into awkward silence, and I couldn't stop my eyes from taking in every one of his features. His dark brown hair was longer in the front, swept to the side in a casual way that made me think he ran his fingers through it often.

Speaking of fingers…

My gaze traveled down to his hands, and a tingle of lust shot through me. He worked with his hands; there was no doubt about that. *I bet they'd be rough to the touch…*

I stopped those thoughts dead in their tracks, heat creeping to my face as I looked away. Why the hell was I checking out another guy when Cameron was asleep in the next room?

Jesus. Just drink your coffee.

The silence between us was thick, and I took a peek at him, but then regretted it. His gaze lingered on my face, intense and curious. Feeling unnerved at the way he was watching me so intently, I decided to break the tension.

Clearing my throat, I said, "So, you're Cameron's roommate?"

"Well, I'm definitely not his lover."

The coffee I had just sipped came sputtering back up, and my face burned with heat as he tossed me a hand towel. I dabbed it at my mouth, wanting to crawl into a hole. "Right. Thanks." Nothing else wanted to come out, and I had to blame the early morning hour on my lack of witty repartee. I sure as hell wasn't about to admit he had me feeling intimidated. *Think, Ryleigh, think. Suck down that coffee, let the caffeine fuel your brain, and come up with something hilarious. Now would be good. Any day now…*

"And you would be?" he asked.

Oh, of course. I'm the stranger sleeping on his couch. Brilliant.

"Ryleigh Phillips," I said. "I went to school with Cameron."

"Oh, right, the reunion. That was last night?"

When I nodded in the affirmative, he cocked his head to the side. "You know, if you'd been my guest, I wouldn't have made you sleep on the couch." He unleashed a full-wattage smile at me then as I sat there, only able to blink.

And wouldn't you know it, right about the time I was staring at him, stupefied, would be the moment

Cameron's bedroom door opened.

Still dressed in the outfit he'd fallen asleep in the night before, Cameron stood in the doorway looking slightly rumpled but nowhere near as rough as I had upon waking. When he saw me, he dropped the hand that had been gripping the back of his neck, his expression somewhere between surprise and relief.

"Hey," he said, a slow grin crossing his face.

I wasn't sure if I was supposed to get up, run out the door, hug him, or what, so I just stayed ass-planted on the stool while I waited for him to make a move. "Hey."

"Hey," the other male voice in the room said, mimicking us, and it hit me then that I hadn't even bothered asking his name.

"Oh what's up, man," Cameron said, walking toward the kitchen bar. He nodded at me. "I see you met Ryleigh."

"Mhmm. I told her it'd be wise to grab coffee before your grumpy ass woke up."

Cameron made a face at me. "He lies. I'm never grumpy."

"Then it doesn't matter if I tell you I took the last of the creamer," his roommate said.

"What?" Cameron picked up the empty creamer bottle from the counter and shook it. "You're a bastard."

Dark-headed guy poured the rest of his coffee into a travel mug and then wiggled his eyebrows. "Enjoy your day, you two. Nice to meet you, Ryleigh."

"Good to meet you too, uh…" I didn't get a chance to ask who he was before he'd grabbed his keys and was out the front door.

"Hunter," Cameron said, filling in his name for me. "Feel free to call him asshole, though." He tossed the empty bottle in the recycling bin before resting his elbows on the counter opposite me. He looked apologetic and a little embarrassed. "I am so, so sorry—"

I waved him off. "No, it's fine. Really. No need to apologize."

"It's just…that's never happened before."

"Well, it's not like we're talking about premature ejaculation." And then I realized what the fuck I'd just said. "Uh…I mean…"

Cameron stared at me for a moment before shaking his head and bursting into laughter. "No, *that* would've been much worse."

My face dropped to my hands and I moaned. "Sorry. Caffeine hasn't kicked in yet."

"Nah, I like this lack of filter. But Ryleigh…" He looked at Hunter's open bedroom door and then back at me. "Where did you sleep last night?"

"AND THEN?"

I tugged at the edge of my apron in an attempt to avoid the three pairs of eyes staring bug-eyed at me. "And then he walked me to my car."

"And then you…?" Shayne asked.

"Went home," I said.

"Wait a minute, can we talk about the fact that he made you sleep on his couch?" Paige's eyebrows were raised up to practically her hairline. "I'm sorry, but in what fucking universe is that acceptable? Why didn't you call Quinn to pick you up?"

"He didn't make me, geez. He passed out and it was late, and I thought maybe…you know. Morning sex."

Shayne cocked an eyebrow. "And did that happen?"

"Well, no. Hunter made me coffee, and then Cameron woke up and…that's it."

"Wait," Quinn interrupted. "You slept in an apartment with two guys and *both* of them had you sleeping on the couch? Jesus, Ryleigh, it's against man-code for that to happen. Did you wear a chastity belt last night or something?"

I groaned, my head falling into my hands. Of course the girls would give me a hard time. I'd been talking up tackling Cameron at the reunion for weeks, so my body wasn't the only one feeling let down.

Still, I was seriously regretting inviting them over for a powwow at my shop during our off hours.

"I think I need another shot of vodka in my Feisty Ho-bag now." Paige pushed her glass stemware toward me, and I grabbed a liquor bottle from behind the bar and tipped some into her glass.

Boozy shakes. They were the bread and butter of Licked during the brunch and evening hours, and the main reason for the expansion next door. I glanced at the black tarp hanging over the doorway that led to the space I'd bought a few months ago and sighed. Construction was running behind, and it was too late to hire another company if I wanted to keep the launch date set.

And I *had* to keep the date set.

"So are you seeing him again?" Shayne asked, dunking her cherry through the layers of baklava bits and whipped cream on top of her Nibble My Nuts shake. "I will totally get involved if I need to."

No doubt she'd be successful. She basically ran one of the top matchmaking companies in the city, not that you'd know it from her degrading pay scale. Her boss was a fucking nightmare, but Shayne was convinced she had to pay her dues.

"I don't need your expert skills this time, but thank you. He's got my number, so…we'll see."

"You can't just wait around for a guy to call," she said.

"I'm not waiting. I've got all that"—I gestured to the ugly tarp that hid the mess behind it—"to deal with, so I'm actually quite busy at the moment."

The three of them gave each other "the look." You know, the one that said, *We've got to help our poor little friend get laid so she doesn't end up gorging on the ice cream and boozy shakes she makes and be relegated to spinsterhood.*

"Guys," I said, placing my hands on the counter as I stood in front of them. "I'm not on my way to spinsterhood. I just have priorities."

"I'm sure you could squeeze Cameron Mathis in," Quinn said with a wink. "Get it? Squeeze him in…"

"More like blow off the dust, grab a key, unlock that shit, and pray there are no bats," Paige agreed.

Oh for fuck's sake. "All right, no more booze for either of you."

"Yeah, yeah, I was done anyway. I've gotta jet." Quinn stood up and grabbed her leather jacket, the one she wore no matter the weather, and slapped down a fifty-dollar bill. "Later, bitches."

Shayne's mouth fell open. "Damn, Quinn. Off to work the corner of Hollywood and Las Palmas?"

"I'm not taking that," I called after Quinn, but she was out the door before it reached her. "One of these days, we're gonna figure out what the hell it is she does."

"And where she gets all that bloody money to blow," Shayne said.

"I'm telling you. Russian spy. All that glossy black hair and badass attitude," Paige said between sips of her shake.

I shrugged. "Nah. Maybe she has a crazy inheritance."

Shayne shook her head. "It should be weird that we don't know how she spends her days or what she does for a living, but—"

"That's Quinn," we all chorused before bursting into laughter.

The store phone rang then, and I answered it with a smile. "Licked Ice Creamery & Booziery."

"May I speak with Ryleigh, please?" The deep voice that filtered through the phone had my body stopping and starting, like when you're on a roller coaster and you get to the top of that first peak and it stops before barreling down at lightening speed and sending your stomach to your feet.

Yeah. Like that.

But the watchful eyes of my friends kept me from

turning into the puddle of goo I knew I would've been had they not been there. I cleared my throat and stood up straighter. "Cameron Mathis. Stalking is illegal in all fifty states."

When Paige and Shayne's eyes widened, I winked at them.

A low chuckle sounded across the line. "Well, you don't answer your cell, and I remembered you work at Licked, so—"

"I own it," I said with my chin up.

"I'm sorry?"

"Licked is my store. I own it, I don't just work here." I didn't mean to sound defensive, but call it a pride thing; I wanted him to know I was a successful businesswoman. That I worked for myself.

"Oh…wow, okay," he said. "Maybe I could come check it out?"

"You could…" A cheesy grin spread across my face, and I turned around before the girls could see it. "Maybe you could stop by this week."

"How's Wednesday?"

"Hmm. I could make that happen."

"Perfect. I'll see you then."

"Bye, Cameron."

I hung up the phone and circled back to my friends.

"Twisting him around your damn finger," Paige said. "High five to that."

As I slapped her hand, my grin grew wider. "I

wouldn't go that far, but—"

The expectant looks on their faces had me reconsidering.

"Okay, yeah I am," I said, picking up my own Slap My Ass and Call Me Sally boozy shake. "Cheers and sayonara, spinsterhood."

WEDNESDAY CAME AROUND, and I'm not ashamed to admit it took me two hours to pick out what I was going to wear that day. Two dozen brightly patterned swing and pencil dresses were scattered across my plush white comforter, making for a dizzying array of choices.

My chestnut hair was already up in my signature updo, and my makeup was heavy on the volumizing mascara and pink gloss. Now all I needed was the perfect dress. Or maybe I should choose my shoes first?

I switched on the light to the walk-in closet and pursed my lips as I ran my fingers across the choices. They stopped on a wine-colored pair of peep-toe heels, and I gingerly lifted them from the shelf and carried them to the bed.

Oooh. They'd go perfectly with the rockabilly dress I'd bought last week. I threw on the ensemble and checked myself out in the full-length mirror on the back of the closet door.

Hmm. Not bad. Not bad at all. A pair of funky earrings, and I was ready to go.

Now, I know what you're thinking, and it's true. I've got pretty eclectic taste. Always have, probably always will. I was wearing vintage dresses even back in high school, which is most likely the reason for my oddball status. But it's amazing how you learn to embrace your awkward as you get older.

I headed down the stairs that led to Licked and flicked off the apartment lights as I went. Yes, I live upstairs from my shop. How convenient, right?

Zoe, my morning manager, right-hand woman, and all-around saint, was already in the kitchen measuring vanilla and pouring it into a bucket.

"Morning, Zoe," I said before tying on an apron. Nodding at the mixture she was prepping, I said, "I do love a fresh batch of Cookie Dil-dough for breakfast."

A chuckle left her as she looked over her shoulder at me. Her lip piercing gleamed under the kitchen lights, and her bouffant 'do, shaved on the sides, was a fresh shade of royal blue. "You do know I only work here because the names of your creams makes it sound like I talk shit all day, right?"

"You do talk shit all day. Names of my creams?" I shook my head. "By the way, dig the hair."

"And that's the second reason I work here. When are you gonna let me give you some fuchsia highlights?"

I took the batch of Up-the-Butt-er Pecan I'd made

yesterday out of the freezer. "I'd rather leave the bright colors to my clothes. And shoes. And face. Pink hair would just be overkill."

"Good point." Zoe popped the lid on the tub of the ice cream she'd just finished making and set it in the blast freezer before taking out another container and following me to the front of the store.

The lights were already on, displaying my penchant for times past covering the space. The floors were black and white checkerboard tile, always gleaming from a fresh wax. The walls alternated between snowy white and rich magenta, and brightly colored frames showcased caricature portraits of not only the ice creams and boozy shakes featured at Licked, but also some of my favorite shining stars from the thirties and beyond, like Laurence Olivier and Rita Hayworth.

I told you. It's my thing.

We set up the featured flavors for the day, and I pulled out all the toppings that had been set from the night before. The theme today was Whack-off Wednesday, and all the flavors would reflect a wacky combination.

Yeah, this isn't any ordinary ice cream shop, if that's what you were thinking. Where would the fun be in that? Exactly. Though who doesn't love ice cream no matter what form, amiright or amiright?

"You're all dressed up today," Zoe said, eyeing my ensemble. Well, what she could see behind the frilly apron with "Get Licked" splashed across the front of it.

"I'm wearing the same thing I always do," I replied.

"No…no, something's different. Did you get laid?"

Sweet…Jesus.

IT WAS WELL past two when Cameron walked through Licked's front door, wearing an immaculately pressed grey business suit that was somehow tailored to his towering frame. I thought again of the Ken dolls I used to play with when I was younger. They never stayed in those suits for long. I had been much too curious about what was underneath all those clothes and then horrified once I realized the answer was—not fucking much.

Aaaand now I'm thinking of him naked. Good job, Ryleigh.

A smile crossed Cameron's lips as he said hello, and his gaze traveled around the shop before landing back on me. "This is amazing. If the food is half as good as the packaging, consider me a lifelong fan."

Oh, the responses I wanted to make to that. But I didn't. I behaved.

"Well, what are you in the mood for?" I asked.

He licked his lips as his eyes scanned the chalkboard menu above me. "Crushed Nuts…Ground-Shaking Orgasm? Decisions, decisions."

"Tell me you're not a double dipper."

"A what?"

My lips tipped up on the side. "A double dipper. Means you're bored with just one and you need the fun of two. Flavors, that is."

Cameron slowly shook his head as he kept his eyes on mine. "I can assure you. I'm more than happy with just one."

I could feel the heat creep up to my cheeks, but I played it cool. Or in my head I did. "That's good to know. So what'll it be?"

"I think..." His eyes went back and forth between the two options. "I think I'd much prefer a Ground-Shaking Orgasm. I'm a sucker for those."

Approved, naughty boy.

"Comin' right up." I smiled and scooped several dark chocolate balls of ice cream into the clear sundae bowl without bothering to ask how many he wanted. He could have the whoooole enchilada. Err, sundae.

After piling it high with crumbles of crispy bacon and topping it with whipped cream and a cherry, I walked over to where he'd been watching me from one of the barstools at the counter, though I suppose his eyes could've been on the dessert in my hands. As I passed Zoe, she inclined her head toward Cameron and mouthed *wow,* which for her was huge—we didn't bat for the same team.

I slid the heavenly concoction his way, and his eyes grew large and hungry. "This might be the best thing I've ever seen in my life," he said. Though proud of my creamery prowess, I admit I wanted him to say it was the *second*-best thing he'd ever seen in his life. You know. After my face. Or my ass.

A huge spoonful went between his lips, and he groaned in pleasure.

Hot damn, is that what he'd sound like in bed? Because hell.

"And it is *definitely* the most delicious thing I've ever had in my mouth," he said around a mouthful of chocolate cream, and I couldn't help but think, *So far...*

That's not too pretentious at all, right?

"I'm glad you like it." I glanced at the register to see Zoe taking care of the customers who'd just walked in and then focused my attention back on Cameron.

He'd already shoveled in a few more spoonfuls, and I had to laugh at his enthusiasm. "Do they not let you out of the office for lunch?"

"No. I meant to come by earlier, but we were slammed. They're trying to get me to fly to Hong Kong to meet with investors there, and—" He stopped himself. "Sorry, that's boring stuff."

"It's not boring if it's something you love. Um...what is it you do again?"

Cameron put down the spoon and laughed. "I work for my father's production company."

"Oh wow. You know, everyone always thought you'd go into the NFL or something."

"Nah. I mean, football was fine for school and stuff, but I've always been interested in the behind the scenes of the movie business. I never really thought about doing anything else."

"I had no idea. And you go on exotic business trips overseas."

"My trips usually entail finding backers for our projects and talking them into giving us millions of dollars from their own pockets. So it's not that exotic, I promise. But…yeah." He shrugged. "I love it. If you cater, maybe we could get you to do our next company event."

"It's a little messy to go on the road," I said, gesturing to his melting ice cream. "But you're more than welcome to have something here any time you want."

"I appreciate that." He smiled, one of those ultra-white, blinding smiles. Then a thought seemed to cross his mind, and he furrowed his brow. "Listen, I have to apologize for the other night—"

"Oh, don't worry about—"

"No," he said, holding his hand up. "My behavior was inexcusable, and, if you'll let me, I'd like to make it up to you."

Ding ding ding. In bed?

I pretended to take a minute to think about his offer before saying, "Yeah, okay. Sure."

His smile came back. "Great. How's tomorrow night?"

Oh damn. I was covering the late shift for the next two nights for one of my staff who had a family emergency. "Actually, I have to wor—" I started before Zoe knocked into me from behind.

"Sorry, boss, I didn't see you there. Hey, I was wondering if I could pick up more hours this week. Like, maybe tomorrow evening?"

That tricky little woman. Bless her.

"You sure you're up for a double shift?" I asked.

Zoe scoffed. "Seriously?"

Yeah, okay. She pretty much lived at the shop anyway. I owed her one.

She winked at me as she walked away, and I turned back to face Cameron.

"I guess it's a date," I said, trying not to cheesy-grin too hard until he left.

"Great. So I'll pick you up…where, exactly?"

"Oh, here's fine. My apartment is upstairs."

"Really? So you weren't kidding when you said you lived at work."

I shook my head. "In more ways than one."

Cameron nodded at the ugly tarp I was hoping he wouldn't notice. Which was like asking someone not to pay attention to an elephant in the room. Maybe I should paint the stupid thing.

"You expanding?" he asked.

"I am. The booziery side of the business has taken on a life of its own, and we need more space. I was hoping it'd be finished by now, but the guys are running so behind, and I'm not sure it'll be done for the Expand Your Empire contest in a couple months."

"Is that the one *Wake Up America* is doing? Damn, that's huge." Cameron gave a low whistle. "So the expansion isn't just limited to next door?"

"Nope. Hoping to take Licked nationwide."

"That's incredible, Ryleigh. You should be proud."

As my eyes wandered the room, taking in all that I'd accomplished so far, I had to agree. "I am."

"You know," he said, looking back at that damn tarp. "I could get Hunter to stop by and take a look, see what's holding up the renovations."

"Oh, you don't need to do that, I'm sure he's booked—"

"No, it's no problem. He owns his own construction business, so maybe he can light a fire under their ass." Cameron winked, and I melted into a puddle. Checking his watch, he stood up and pulled a few bills out of his pocket before pushing them my way. "I've got to get back to the office, but I'll pick you up tomorrow at, say, seven?"

"Seven's perfect. And it's on the house," I said, shaking my head at his attempt to pay. He stuffed the bills into the tip jar on the counter and gave me one last gorgeous smile before heading out the door.

As the deliciousness that was Cameron walked out, a new recipe took hold in my mind. *A Sex God Sundae: a king-size banana split, salty nuts, extra cream…*

Chapter Five
Scooping Balls

THE NEXT DAY, I was scooping balls of Like a Virgin vanilla bean into a Coke Whore float when the front door chimed, and in walked Cameron's roommate. *Hunter*. Sporting another pair of worn jeans that sat on his hips and looked like they'd been dark to begin with.

He looked… Well. *Fucking hot.* Not that I had noticed.

Okay, fine, so I noticed. It was hard not to with the way he sauntered into my shop. I handed the Coke float to the last customer in line and then wiped my hands on a wet towel.

"Let me guess," I said. "Your Ass is Grass?"

When he raised an eyebrow at me, I noticed how impossibly long his lashes were. Why do guys always get the perfect ones, and women have to pay for them?

"Excuse me?" he said.

I shrugged. "You look like a mint chocolate chip with brownies kind of guy."

"And what makes you say that?"

"It's my job to know these things."

He smirked and then glanced around the store. "Cameron mentioned you needed help with renovations."

"I've got some guys on it already, but they seem to be taking their sweet-ass time."

When Hunter's eyes landed on the tarp, he inclined his head. "They working today?"

"Should be."

He walked over and lifted the edge of the cover to peer into the workspace. Over his shoulder, he asked, "Mind if I go in?"

"No, give me a sec and I'll join you." I untied the apron I'd chosen to match my burgundy swing dress and placed it on a hook. "Be right back," I told my staff.

I followed Hunter into the empty space next door, the smell of woodcuttings greeting my nose.

"How long have they been on the job?" he asked as he walked slowly around the room, taking in every inch of the space from wall to ceiling. It was a mess. Even I could see that. It would've been in better shape just to leave it like the retail store it had been than to have them tear it all apart so it was a big pile of nothing.

"About four weeks. I'd given them a deadline of less

than six weeks from now, but, uh"—I sidestepped tools scattered on the ground—"I'm thinking that won't happen."

When Hunter had walked around the entire interior, he came back to where I was standing at the missing bar space. His lips were pursed and he crossed his arms over his chest. "Won't happen," he confirmed.

My heart sank. I needed this expansion to go through because the *Wake Up America* special would be filmed here, and a huge part of whether I could spin Licked off into a chain hinged on how it went. I'd been trying not to let myself think my timeline had been unreasonable and they wouldn't get it done. Big fucking mistake.

"Oh God," I said with a groan, rubbing my forehead. "What do I do? How do I make them go faster?"

"Who's the contractor?"

"Scott Lewiston."

"I could've guessed that. Where are they now?"

"Um...extended lunch break, if I had to guess."

He shook his head. "Tell me what you've got going on here."

I led him back around the room, showing him where the bar would be, how I envisioned the high-top tables, the booths, and the private room and gaming area in the back. It would be the same vibe as Licked, but catered toward the night crowd.

Licked...After Dark.

"All right," Hunter said when I'd finished giving him the tour. "I'll do it."

"What?" I sputtered. "I can't let you do that."

"That would be a stupid move on your part."

"We have a contract—"

"I'll get you out of it. And then my team will take over." His voice brooked no argument, but I did anyway. Because I can be a persistent pain in the ass.

"But...how...why would you do that? I've never even seen your work before."

"My guys are all on break right now, but they get antsy when I make them take a forced vacation. We can have this done by your deadline. And you've been to our place, so you *have* seen my work."

I stared at him in shock. "That all sounds great, but why would you do this for me? You don't even know me."

Hunter's head cocked to the side as he studied my face, and when his eyes were on my mouth, I shivered. Must've been a draft from the open tarp.

"You need help, right?" he asked, his arms still crossed, his biceps bulging against the material of his grey shirt. That answered the question, *Do you work out? Damn.*

Swallowing, I said, "Yeah. Yeah, I think I do."

He gave a curt nod and started to back away. "I'll draft up the contract and bring it by tomorrow. I'll get the blueprints from Scotty boy."

"Wait. What should I do about them—"

Hunter's eyes were intense on mine. "I'll take care of it. They'll be out by the end of the day."

And then he was gone.

THURSDAY EVENING HAD arrived, and I'd begged Paige to help me find something fabulous to wear. And by fabulous, I also mean *fuckable.*

"I'm thinking the black pencil dress. Definitely." Paige's appraising eye ran down the length of one of the outfits I held in my hands. "And those candy-apple heels. Bam. Done."

"You're the best," I said, tossing the other outfit on the bed and shimmying into the winning number.

"Wait. Are you wearing those?" she asked, indicating my matching satin bra and panties.

"What's wrong with these?"

Paige rolled her eyes and pushed off the bed before strolling over to my dresser. She pulled open the top drawer and rummaged around before holding up a thong. "This. Wear this."

"That's not gonna hold anything in," I protested.

"You don't have anything to *hold* in, so will you please just put it on." Tossing the underwear to me, she went and flopped back on the bed. "Where's he taking you?"

"No idea."

"Oooh, surprises. Maybe he'll take you to Shellan's. I've been dying to go there."

"Yeah, and the wait list is about three months long." Pulling on the thong I'd never worn, I felt naked. "I think I'm gonna pass on these. With any luck, he won't even notice what I'm wearing under my skirt because he'll be too busy ripping it off."

"With his teeth, and trust me, thongs are the better option. Hipster panties are not gonna get you hitched. You don't bust those out until after marriage. Trust me on this."

Leave it to the wedding coordinator to be thinking that far ahead. *Fine.* The damn thong would stay. "Have I ever mentioned how weird it is that you of all people plan weddings for a living? You're the most anti-commitment person I've ever met."

"Hey, that's not true. I commit for a whole week sometimes."

I snorted as I pulled the SJP heels off the rack and slid them on. Admiring my reflection, I said, "That's a rarity and you know it. What I don't understand is how you manage to spout all the ooey-gooey love stuff all day long."

"My gag reflex is amazing," Paige replied, waggling her eyebrows before dodging the clutch I threw at her. She laughed. "Well, it's true."

"When are you just gonna admit you're madly in love with Dawson and settle down and pop out a soccer team already?"

Now it was her turn to throw the clutch.

"Double Dick? He's an imbecile. I wouldn't fuck him if he changed his name to Prince Harry and bought out

Tiffany's."

Sure she wouldn't. Richard Dawson and Paige had been playing the love-hate game for years now, and each was determined that the other was the lowest, most disgusting human they'd ever come across in their entire existence. We humored her because it was entertaining as all hell to watch, but it would surprise no one if we learned they were hate-fucking behind the scenes. We'd already placed bets.

My cell rang then—Cameron letting me know he was waiting at the front. When I ended the call, I took a deep breath and faced Paige. "So? What do you think?"

"Entirely fuckable. Go get 'em, tiger."

IT HAD BEEN a nice night. Emphasis on *nice.*

Cameron had taken me to The Oyster House overlooking the Pacific, and we'd talked about what we'd been up to since we graduated, about our families, our interests. It was all just so…nice.

I know, I keep saying that word, but…well, maybe I expected more. Like passion and sparks and heavy sexual tension. Our conversation hadn't screamed *I can't wait to get you tangled in my sheets,* but there was still time.

After dinner, we'd walked down to the beach, and he'd grabbed my hand as I held my shoes in my other. The breeze was chillier than I expected, and, gentleman that he was, he gave me his coat. It was warm and smelled like him—fresh, clean…like spring rain. And it was long, considering his height, which I was grateful for. It stopped my teeth from chattering, at least.

"I'm glad you said yes to tonight," Cameron said, squeezing my hand. "After my last impression, I wouldn't have blamed you for turning me down."

"It's not your fault you're narcoleptic." I looked up and gave him a half-smile. "Although if you pull that act while we're on this beach, I'll be tempted to leave you here."

He laughed and nodded. "Fair enough."

When he stopped and pulled on my hand, I backtracked to face him. His hands went to my waist, his gorgeous eyes on mine, and I saw it. The I'm-gonna-kiss-you-now-so-you'd-better-buckle-up look.

My heart thumped loudly in my chest, and suddenly, I was aware of every little thing: how cold I was, how much I wished I'd worn pants and a sweater, how much I needed to actually go *buy* pants and a sweater, the loud roar of the ocean, the other couples that passed us that were out for a romantic stroll, that I wished I'd worn a clear gloss instead of my signature pink because it was going to smear if he kissed me…

Kissed me.

My stomach twisted in knots, and my head swam.

Oh no. This was not how this was supposed to go. I wasn't supposed to be nervous with dread. I was supposed to be nervous from excitement.

Ryleigh, this is what you've wanted. Look at that face. Who wouldn't want to kiss those perfect lips? I begged myself to get it together so I could enjoy this. I *was* going to enjoy this, dammit. Because I couldn't forever be known as the girl who passed out when Cameron Mathis kissed her.

His eyes searched mine, and he must've seen something there, because he asked, "Are you okay?"

"I'm more than okay." Liar. *I'm such a liar.* I rested my hands on his chest as his brow furrowed.

"Are you sure? Because your teeth are chattering."

They were? *Shit. Pull it together, teeth. Cameron's about to warm your mouth up in three…two…one…*

As I inclined my head and leaned forward, fat raindrops landed on my face.

What the hell?

My eyes blinked open, and I saw drops smacking Cameron in the face too. And not just any raindrops. Cold-as-a-toilet-seat-in-an-igloo drops.

As soon as the thought crossed my mind, the skies opened up, and in seconds we were drenched. *Drenched.* In Southern California. Where rain is obsolete, and a heavy downpour is a smattering of sprinkles. Until tonight.

Cameron's hold on my waist left as he grabbed my hand, both of us running through the dunes of sand back to his car. My shivering wasn't just limited to my teeth anymore, as my body was racked with shaking.

Hello, Mother Nature. It's me, Ryleigh. Thanks for giving

me a break with the panic attack, but next time, could you at least let him kiss me first? I just needed to get the first one out of the way, and then I'd be okay.

At least that was what I hoped.

He put the heater on blast once we got inside the car and then began the drive back to my place. Even the seats began to warm up, and for that, I was grateful. Once my body stopped convulsing, *and God, isn't that sexy,* I relaxed into the seat, letting the warmth envelop me.

Cameron glanced over and smiled. "Better?"

"Much better."

"Good."

I wondered if he'd reach across the console and grab my hand. Did I want him to? *What the hell, Ryleigh?* Of course I did. Or I could just grab his. No, I'm not that bold. I'd probably reach for it and grab his crotch instead. Um, again.

"Hunter mentioned he'll be taking over the renovations for your place," Cameron said. He ran his hand over his wet face and hair. It was still styled perfectly in place, just glistening from the rain now. His chiseled face was picture perfect, even soaking wet.

How the hell was it fair he looked like he'd just shot an Abercrombie ad under rain hoses and I looked like a drowned rat? Okay, so I hadn't looked at myself yet, but I knew it was true. When I'd run my hand over my hair, the elaborate updo I'd spent an hour on had sagged like a deflated party balloon.

I swiped my fingers under my eyes to get rid of my non-waterproof and probably now dripping mascara. "Yeah, he starts tomorrow. He moves quick. I can't believe he was able to take over from Scott."

"You don't know Hunter. When he puts his mind to something, he's tenacious."

"Well, he's saving my ass, so thank you. Free ice cream for life any time you come in."

"I'm not even going to pretend to turn that down." Cameron pulled into an open space in front of my shop/apartment, and shut off the car. The rain was pelting the vehicle, the streams running down the windows becoming a shield from the outside. With Cameron shifting to face me, it was suddenly too dark, too warm, too enclosed. The guy couldn't win for trying. The nervousness I'd felt on the beach returned.

Damn nerves. Go away.

It wasn't like I hadn't kissed guys. I had. A million guys. Or at least twenty. Just call me a kiss-o-holic. I was damn good, and I could blow Cameron's mind. If only I could make myself move the ten inches closer and attack his mouth.

He seemed to sense my hesitation, and pulled back. "So," he said. "I'll be leaving tomorrow morning for Hong Kong. It looks like I'll be gone at least a couple of weeks if all goes well…"

Ah, there it was. Disappointment pushing away my nerves. Fucking finally.

"Make sure to eat some roast duck for me."

He chuckled. "Yeah, I'll do that." Running his hand over the steering wheel, he didn't look at me as he asked, "So…can I see you again? When I get back?"

"I'd like that," I said, my lips tipping up in a smile.

"Yeah?"

"Definitely."

Cameron looked at me then, his light eyes shining in the dark interior. He leaned toward me, his intention clear.

Oh hell. We're doing this. I'm *doing this.*

I mimicked his movement, my head inclining to the right at the same time his moved in the same direction. It startled me so much I burst out laughing.

"Um…I can go this way," I said, pointing to the left.

He grinned. "Either way." Taking my face in his hands, he leaned down slowly, his smile broadening when my head moved to the left. And then closer…closer…until I felt the warmth of his breath on my li—

BLEEP. BLEEP. BLEEP. BLEEP. BLEEP. BLEEP. BLEEP. BLE—

We both jerked back, the car alarm next to us going off at an ear-splitting volume.

Yeah. This was not gonna happen tonight.

With a sigh, I picked up my clutch from the floorboard. "I should probably go check on things inside," I said, nodding at Licked. It was past closing time, and of course Zoe would've done a perfect job of closing things up, but it felt like a good excuse. We'd just start over when he got back from Hong Kong. "I'll see you when you get back?"

Cameron nodded, giving me a smile, but he looked a little disappointed. Or maybe I was projecting. I wanted him to feel disappointed. *Hmm, maybe that can work in my favor.* Disappointment could turn into missing me madly, and he'd probably jump me when he got back in town. The girls would be so excited. And, of course, so would I.

"You can count on it," he said. "Let me walk you to the door." He reached for his door handle, and I laid my hand on his arm.

"No need for you to get soaked again. I'm just gonna make a run for it." When he didn't look convinced, I said, "Really. I already know you're a gentlemen." And then I jumped out of the car and dashed for the door, not bothering to turn back until I was inside the private entrance that led to my apartment.

No need for his last glimpse of me to be a soggy mess. I'd rather him think of me as the hot woman he couldn't wait to come back to and do all sorts of inappropriate things with. *Yeah,* let him think on that while he was gone.

Chapter Six
Cinderfuckinrella

"*THAT'S* YOUR NEW contractor? Bloody hell." Shayne's eyes were wide as she watched Hunter giving instructions to his crew. By the way she was eyeballing him, I had a feeling I'd have to kick her out of the shop soon.

"Aren't you a few hours late for work?" I asked, wiping down the already clean countertops. I wasn't about to admit it, but I was keeping an eye on those guys too. One specifically. But just to make sure he wasn't a lazy good-for-nothing like the last guy.

Oh yeah. And Hunter had replaced the black tarp with a clear one. He said it was for transparency reasons, meaning I could check in at any time and make sure they weren't sitting around having a beer.

But as I checked out his crew, a mix of guys aged

twenty to fortyish, I thought maybe that wasn't the whole reason. It was like he'd found the Magic Mike crew of construction. Which made Hunter...Channing Tatum. But no, that wasn't completely accurate. With his tousled brown hair, olive skin, and intense eyes, he was more like James Dean's older brother. I bit down hard on my lip.

"...just here to check your schedule. Hello? Ryleigh?" Shayne waved her hand in front of my face, and I snapped out of my stupor.

"What?"

Her gaze followed mine to where Hunter was looking right at me. And his eyes on mine snapped me back to reality, and I quickly looked away.

"Sorry, what were you saying?" I asked. "Check my schedule for what?"

Shayne's eyebrow went up. "Isn't that Cameron's roommate? The one staring at you?"

I didn't bother looking to see who she meant. Or if he was still looking at me. "Yeah, apparently so. So you were saying—"

"He's *hot*. Holy cow." Shayne fanned herself with her hand. "I don't know how you plan to get any work done with the Chippendales over there."

Rolling my eyes, I wiped the counter with a little more vigor. "I do have world domination plans to deal with, so I think I'll be a little preoccupied."

She laughed. "Of course you do. So how's this Sunday night for a mixer? I know it's Wednesday and less than a week notice is crazy last-minute, but you know—"

"Val," I said, shaking my head. "You have the most demanding, psychotic boss in the world, you know that, right?"

"Girl's gotta do what a girl's gotta do. She's entertaining, at the very least."

"She's a pill-popping sexual deviant diva whore."

"True."

"She sets you up with all the client rejects as 'interviews.'"

"And there's that."

"And what about the time she made you go to her house to FedEx her favorite pair of panties to her while she was on vacation?"

Shayne laughed. "That too." She ran her hands over her long, curly red locks, the kind that made you think of the quintessential feisty Irish lass—which was far from what she actually was.

A sweet Australian transplant, that's what she was. She'd been such a quiet thing when she'd first arrived in L.A., all bright-eyed with an accent everyone fainted over, but after a decade in the U.S., she'd been thoroughly corrupted and lost most of the loony Aussie words we didn't understand, though she could pull them back out when she needed to. And damn, did the boys love that.

I grabbed my appointment book from behind the counter and looked at this week's schedule. Not that I didn't already know it, but it never hurt to double-check myself.

We closed the shop Sunday evenings and Mondays, leaving it open for private parties and events, and if we didn't have those—a much-needed break. Shayne worked with one of the top matchmaking companies in the city, and they frequently held mixers at Licked. I loved it—watching all that first-date awkwardness was entertaining as hell.

"Sunday works," I said, tossing the appointment book back in its spot.

"You're a goddess." Shayne leaned over the bar and grabbed me in a tackle hug. "I'll make sure to tell Val last-minute bookings require a twenty percent surcharge."

"No complaints about that. Want a shake to go?"

"Nah, I have a feeling I'll be stopping by quite a bit over the next few weeks. You know. For the view." She looked back at the guys working next door and grinned.

I swiped her with my dishrag. "Out, you perv. Go slack somewhere else."

She waved as she left, and her timing was perfect. We were slammed with a rush of customers for a good three hours straight, several of them asking for flavors reserved for our Friday night 'Flavors from Your Favorite Flicks' theme. That day always proved to be a popular one. I mean, who could resist buying a Bleedin' Armadillo Grooms Cake shake or a Cinderfuckinrella sundae?

When it slowed, I took the opportunity to go next door to check things out and make sure there were no issues. It'd been a steady mix of drills and hammering throughout the day, so I wasn't worried, though I'd had to turn up the music in the shop to help drown it out a bit.

Hunter was in the middle of sawing a long piece of wood when he looked over at me. He held up his hand for me to stay where I was, and then set down the saw and grabbed a hardhat and goggles from the set lined against the wall. Handing them to me, he said, "No entering without one."

"It'll smash my hair."

He gave me a look I didn't dare argue with, and I sighed before donning the glasses and gently placing the bright yellow hat on my head, holding on to it so it didn't sit completely on my curls.

"How come you're not wearing a hat?"

"Because I'm the boss."

"That's not a good reason. I'm not paying workman's comp when you get knocked out by a flying hammer."

"I've got a strict policy about tools in the workplace. They don't fly."

"Good, then I won't have to worry about your brain damage. That's a weight off." I looked around at their progress, noting that even though it'd only been half a day, they were almost done knocking down everything that needed to go. It had taken the other crew weeks to do half that. Once again, I kicked myself for not busting their balls. "So how's it going?" I asked.

As Hunter launched into the spiel about what they'd been doing, I caught myself paying more attention to his mouth than what was coming out of it. A very stupid thing to do, because he soon noticed.

"Your eyes are glazing over," he said.

"What?" I knew what he meant, but he was wrong about the why.

"Sorry, I won't bore you with the details if you don't want to know."

"No, no, that's... This is great. Progress. You guys are on top of it. Really."

Hunter's brow creased as if he were trying to decide if I was being sincere, and then it smoothed out. "Well, we've got a long way to go, but we'll get it done. I do have a question about the seating arrangements." He walked over to where the blueprint was taped to the wall and pointed. "With the seating area, you're going to want to make this path right here a little wider or it'll be too cramped for people to walk to the back area easily. Maybe if you made the high-tops a bit smaller, like for two people instead of four, it'd save you a ton of space."

Slowly nodding, I said, "That makes sense, but Scott ordered the tables weeks ago."

"Scott ordered them?"

"Yeah. I mean, I guess we could call the company and see if they can switch them out for a smaller version."

Hunter stared at me. "Right...yeah, okay, I'll check into that."

I smiled. "Great. Good catch. I wasn't even thinking about how wide the walkway would actually be. I was more focused on the front of the store. Thanks."

He nodded slowly. "No problem. I'd better get back to it, but I'll, uh, keep you posted on the tables."

"Perfect." I removed the hat and glasses and handed them to him, and then patted my hair to make sure it wasn't a complete mess.

"It still looks good," Hunter said, as he backed away. "Your hair. It all looks"—he scanned the rest of my body before looking back at my face—"really good."

As I stood there, frozen, he picked up the saw from the bar and went back to cutting through the wood. I tried not to notice the strong muscles in his back as he—

Move. Move your feet, Ryleigh.

With an awkward shuffle, I made my way back to the other side of the tarp, also now known as my safe haven. I took in a deep lungful of sweet-scented air, the cheerful room a welcome change from the testosterone-filled space.

"Everything good next door?" Zoe asked, as I tied my apron back on and washed my hands.

"Gonna be breathtaking."

Zoe bumped my hip with hers. "I wasn't referring to him."

"Who?" I asked, knowing good and full well whom the hell she meant.

"That dark-headed one with the dreamy eyes."

"The dreamy... Oh Lord, not you too."

"I'm not mooning over the guy, but I can appreciate an attractive specimen when I see one."

"Mhmm. Sure." I grabbed a clean stack of glass

sundae dishes and carried them to the front counter as Zoe followed.

"If you need to test him out, I can cover another evening shift—"

After setting down the dishes, I whirled around. "Wait a minute. Just the other day you were telling me to take the night off to go on a date with Cameron. That's his *roommate*, Z."

"Yeah, and then I saw the way you flushed when that Hunter guy walked in."

"I didn't flush," I said, turning my back on her. "There was no flushing."

"Whatever you say. I'm guessing it's just the temperature that has your cheeks all pink right now."

As Zoe took over the register, I spun away and put the back of my hand up to my cheek. It did feel a little warm, but that didn't have anything to do with a guy. Especially an off-limits one I had absolutely no interest in.

Riiiiiiight.

I WAS DOING inventory when Hunter came walking into my shop Friday afternoon. He always stayed on the After Dark side, so that was my first clue that something wasn't right. My second clue was the look on his face.

Mentally preparing myself for whatever it was he wanted to dump on me, I held the notepad to my chest and plastered a smile on my face as he walked up to the register.

"Please tell me you don't have bad news," I said through my teeth.

Hunter frowned. "What's wrong with your face?"

"What do you mean?"

"Is that some kind of Botox shit?"

I let my smile drop. "No, it's not some kind of Botox…anything, and watch your mouth around my customers." When I realized what I just said, I shook my head. "Sorry, I sounded like my grandma just then. And it's not like I don't sell ice cream that's called worse."

"No, you're right." He made the motion of zipping his lips.

Chimes went off as the front door opened, and a pair of twenty-somethings entered the store.

"Hey there. Ready to Get Licked?" I said in greeting, which earned high-pitched giggles from them and a raised eyebrow from Hunter. There was a wicked gleam in his eyes, and I nodded at him to take a seat at the bar. Turning back to the women, I asked, "First time here?"

"Yeah, our coworker told us about this place and said we had to come," the first girl with shaggy blond hair said. She looked around the store with an approving eye. "This is so rad. I love the colors." Then she looked at the bright pink and aqua rockabilly dress I was sporting today. "And you match. Is this your store?"

I glanced down at my outfit and laughed. "Yeah, I suppose that's obvious. What can I make for you ladies today? One of the specials today is a Dammit Spike from Notting Hill."

Their eyes went big and round.

"We're a little unconventional here," I said with a wink.

"That's cool," the blond said before turning to her friend. "What was that she told us to get? Something salted caramel?"

"I thought it had candy in it?" her friend said.

"You mean the S&M&M?" I asked. "Salted caramel ice cream with two handfuls of M&M's? Sound about right?"

"Yeah," the blond said with a chuckle. "That's it. But just two small ones."

I smiled at her and swiped the card she handed to me. "Comin' right up."

After putting together their sundaes and letting Amber and Heather, two of my employees, cover the counter, I went over to where Hunter was seated at the far end on a barstool.

Though he'd been working for hours, he wasn't a sweaty mess like he should've been. No dirty construction guys over here. This reaffirmed Shayne's Chippendales theory.

"Okay, tell me," I said, stopping in front of him and crossing my arms, as if that would somehow act as a barrier for whatever the bad news was. *Please let them be able to finish on time. Please please please.*

Hunter rubbed the stubble on his jaw and sighed. "I need you to promise you won't freak out. There's always a solution."

"You're asking me to promise I won't freak out when you know I have a reason to or you wouldn't be telling me that. Spit it out."

"The orders you gave to Scott were not put through."

I blinked. "What? What does that mean?"

"It means the tables, the chairs, the lighting fixtures, the bar…none of that has been ordered."

"What! Oh my God."

"I said don't freak out."

"Don't tell me not to freak out. What did he do, buy a house in the Bahamas with the money? Oh my God."

"Hey, keep your voice down." He inclined his head at a few customers close by who were watching my meltdown and then looked back at me, his lips tipping up in a grin as he threw my earlier words back in my face.

"Sorry about that," I said, addressing the customers and putting on a smile before pointing at the tarp. "You know. Renovations." When they went back to eating, I white-knuckled the counter. "I think I'm gonna pass out."

"You're not gonna pass out," Hunter said, standing up. "Can we go to your office or somewhere more private to discuss this?"

I moaned. "I don't have an office. And now I don't have furniture. Or lights. I'll have to serve everyone in plastic cups by candlelight while they sit on the floor."

"All right, stay there." Hunter rounded the end of the bar and grabbed my elbow, his other hand on my lower back as he helped me and my wobbly legs to an empty booth. I plopped down, super ladylike, on the hot-pink vinyl and scooted to the middle before dropping my head in my hands.

"Do you need a paper bag?" he asked, as he sat down across from me.

"No. Just…you said there's always a solution. I'm gonna need to hear that right now before I go drown myself in a vat of ice cream."

"Look at me."

"That's not a solu—"

"Look at me." His voice was demanding this time, and I lifted my head to see eyes intense on mine. Intense and yet comforting. Like just gazing at them set my mind more at ease and had the tension escaping my body.

How does he do that? Does he have some kind of mood stabilizer superpower or something?

Apparently I said that last part out loud, because he chuckled. "Not that I know of, but I'm glad to see I have that kind of effect on you."

For some reason, that made me squirm. Relaxed wasn't the only effect he had on my traitorous body, it seemed. Which pissed me off.

"Okay, I'm looking at you, what now?" I said. "Is this where you convince me it's not the end of the world, and we can bring in plastic chairs if we have to and call it chic?"

Hunter leaned forward and clasped his hands together. Rough, manly hands, the kind that knew their way around…well, probably everything. I shivered.

"I wanted you to look me in the eye and believe me when I tell you we've got this. I won't lie, though. Your orders are fucked. There's no way on your timeline to get any of those pieces custom-made and shipped in time. It's just not gonna happen."

"Oh my G—"

"But I've got a better idea. I think I get the look you're going for, and there's a place near Palm Desert that makes incredible one-of-a-kind pieces. I know the owner, and he can guarantee having them done when you need them. It's just a matter of picking out what you like."

"That's, like, three hours away. Do they have a website or a catalog I can look at first?"

Hunter shook his head. "He's a bit old-school, but that's exactly why he's great for this project. And no, I don't get some kind of commission for referring, I just know his work. Up to you how you want to move forward."

"So you're saying I have to go to his shop?"

"Yeah. He's out of town, so how's next weekend?"

I flipped the pages of the calendar in my mind. "The weekend works, but since we're closed on Mondays, can I do it then?"

"Sure thing. I'll just check with Mitch and make sure it's good with him too."

"Thank you, but what's this 'we' business?"

"You can't just go pick out whatever you want with no regard to my side of things—"

"*Your* side of things?" I interrupted.

"Well, my business eye. Plus, I can get you a better rate if I'm there."

"Right. You're right. And this place can do what I envision for the pieces? Like unusual flairs—"

"Even better, no doubt."

I looked at him warily, but he seemed confident about it, and he hadn't steered me wrong yet. I blew out a breath. "Thank you. You're saving my ass yet again."

With a shrug, Hunter said, "Not a problem. It's a nice ass." When my mouth fell open, he chuckled. "But I should probably get back to it." He slid out of the booth and looked down at me. "You need any help?"

"What, standing up? Nah, I think the urge to dive into a tub of whipped cream has passed."

A sinful look crossed Hunter's face then. "That's too bad," he said quietly, rapping his knuckles on the table before walking away.

What the hell was that supposed to mean? He wanted me to drown myself in whipped cream or he wanted to see me in—

Oh. Oh damn. This guy was potent, and if that sexy glint in his eyes was anything to go by, it was pretty clear he knew it, too.

THE NEXT MORNING as I was walking in the shop after having made a run for coffee beans, Hunter strolled through the tarp.

I gave him a sharp look as I rounded the counter and shook my head. "Nope. No way. Don't even say it."

He stopped, holding his hands up, and I tried not to look at the way the red shirt he wore with his company's logo across the front sculpted to his muscles.

"What'd I do?" he asked.

"Nothing yet, but I'm sure you're coming to tell me something I don't want to hear."

"Now why would you think that?"

"Is it the plumbing this time? Or the furniture guy has closed his business permanently and I'll have to get those plastic chairs after all? Or is it termites? Please don't say termites. I think I could handle anything else."

"It's not termites."

"Oh thank you, God. The plumbing?"

"Is fine," Hunter said as he came around to the front register.

"So this is just a friendly hello?"

"It is."

"Oh. Well, hi."

"Hey." He smiled, and while his wasn't the beaming smile of Cameron's, it was something worse. Much worse. It was sexy with a side of cocky, one that no doubt had women flinging their panties in his direction. But not me. Nope. I was holding on to my hipsters, thankyouverymuch.

"Can I get you and your guys drinks or anything?"

"No, thanks. We don't usually have vodka until after lunch."

"What?"

He laughed. "Not on duty, of course."

"Right." The feeling in my stomach could only be described as anxious, the casual hellos scaring me more than the possibility of termites. Okay, now *that* was a problem.

He cleared his throat and glanced up at the menu. "So, I've had to smell your shop for a week now, and I have to say"—he looked at me and leaned in closer—"fucking delicious."

"Um." Dammit, why was my face getting hot? This was why I needed a tan. Pasty-white girl who blushes easy gave me away too much. Great. "Thank you."

"I thought maybe I could have a taste?"

My eyes were on his lips, which were closer than they were a few seconds ago. Or was I imagining things? "I don't think that's a good idea," I mumbled.

"Why not? No one's here."

"Because…" My mind tried to come up with a logical reason, but I couldn't seem to focus on anything but his damn lips. "Because Cameron's your roommate."

"What does that have to do with trying out this famous ice cream I've heard so much about?"

When I looked away from his mouth, it hit me what he was saying. Oh come *on*—

"What did you think I meant?" he asked, his eyes smirking at me.

There was no way my face wasn't pinker than my pencil dress. *Please, God. If that massive earthquake everyone keeps talking about is going to happen in my lifetime, can it be now? Can it just swallow me whole, right here, right now?*

Because fuck.

"Which would you like to try?" I asked, my lame attempt at changing the subject all I could think to do besides run away like a little girl.

His smile grew bigger. "Oh, I think *you* should tell *me* what you'd like me to try."

"Feel free to eeny meeny miny moe it if that helps."

"So you can't give me a recommendation?"

"Oh, I could. I was just about to switch out the specials from yesterday's specials, so hmm… The Wanker is right up your alley."

"Ouch. You know," he said, leaning in again as if telling me a secret, "I wouldn't be so polite if we weren't talking about ice cream."

He couldn't be serious. Flirting with me after that embarrassing denial? I wasn't giving in to *that* discussion. Hell no. "All right, Stage Five Clinger it is."

"I'll go with Ravaged Raw," he said, pulling out his wallet, to which I held up my hand to stop him.

"And what size?"

"Just a scoop is fine."

I nodded. "Sure thing. One Castrated Ball of Ravaged Raw for Mr. Morgan." I held up the scooper like a weapon and gave an evil smile. I couldn't stop myself from doing it every time someone ordered a one-scooper, even if they soon changed their minds.

"Wait—what? I don't want a castrated ball."

"But you said just one scoop. One scoop, one ball.

Unless you'd like a full set?"

Hunter just shook his head at me. "You're a sick, twisted woman."

"Thank you," I said with a smile.

"What's two scoops?"

"Well, two scoops would be the full set of Love Balls."

"Yeah, let's go with that," he said, adjusting his jeans.

"Wise choice."

And that, ladies and gentlemen, is why it's called the Castrated Ball. No one wants to order it, so it's always an upsell. I can be a genius when I want to be. The rest of the time I'm just making a fool of myself in front of gorgeous guys.

No—not gorgeous. Annoying.

"So is this always what you wanted to do?" Hunter asked when I pushed his order across the table. "Open an ice cream shop?"

I set about getting the front end ready for opening the shop as I answered his questions. "Yep. My grandparents owned one in Newport, and I always thought it was the coolest thing growing up. That, and I have an insatiable sweet tooth."

"That'd be my weakness too," Hunter said with a wink. "Cam mentioned you were always into this style back in school."

"What, the retro thing?"

He nodded. "And the outfits."

"Yeah, I wasn't the most popular kid for it, but..." I shrugged. "I mean, you like what you like. Maybe it was growing up in my grandparents' shop that rubbed off on me, but I was just obsessed with everything from the forties, fifties, and sixties. I thought the women were beautiful and the men were so debonair. So classic. I guess it just...stuck with me."

"I like that. The not caring what anyone else thinks."

"Oh, I cared. You think hearing whispers in the hallway doesn't wear on your self-confidence when you're fifteen? It totally does. I got so upset that I made my mom take me shopping for jeans. I wore those for about a week and went home crying every single day. It just wasn't me. Wasn't worth it." I clamped my mouth shut. Okay, where had all *that* come from?

Hunter's eyes were pensive as he looked me over. "You're different."

"So?"

"Different looks good on you."

I bit down hard on my lip to keep from acknowledging his compliment with a smile. "Thank you."

He took another bite of his ice cream, and I busied myself with prepping the theme toppings for the day. But when a hard knock on the door sounded moments later, I looked up and groaned.

"Oh no," I said when I saw who it was.

Hunter followed my gaze. "Want me to tell her you're not open yet?"

"No." Sighing, I made my way around the bar. "It's my best friend Shayne's boss. Val. Runs a matchmaking company and is a nightmare like you wouldn't believe."

I set about unlocking the door, and then opened it wide, putting a smile on my face. "Val. What brings you by?"

The woman breezed by me, all Chanel No. 5 and a fur wrap, even in the middle of July. She was a tall, broad woman with a permanent red lip, and a husky voice that would've kicked Kathleen Turner's ass in a round of "Who's got the better sex operator voice?" Though she had to be pushing fifty, there wasn't a wrinkle to be seen anywhere. A stretched and injected piece of work, this one.

"I heard about the renovations, and I wanted to make sure there wouldn't be any nailing going on during our mixer tomorrow. Well," she said with a smirk, "no *unauthorized,* non-paying nailing."

"Everything's all set, and the crew is off tomorrow, so no need to worry."

Val wrinkled her nose and walked over to the tarp. "What the hell do you call this? I need you to get rid of it."

"And…do what, exactly?" I asked.

Val looked at me as if she couldn't understand why I wasn't saying, "Yes, ma'am, anything for you, ma'am." She blew out a haughty breath, and then her eyes landed on Hunter. They grew bigger when she saw his face before narrowing when she caught sight of what he was wearing.

"You," she said, snapping her fingers. "Please help

Ryleigh understand that this isn't going to do for my event. Trashy, not classy."

I almost snorted. As if that woman would know classy if it walked up and whacked her on the nose with a vintage cigarette holder.

Hunter turned on his barstool to face Val, his face impassive. "Maybe we could find a tarp with glitter to put up for the night. How's that sound?"

"There will be no tarps *or* glitter, unless one of my clients has a fetish for them, in which case, you can keep them stocked in the back."

"I'm guessing a beaded curtain is out of the question too?" Hunter asked.

"Unless it's made out of diamonds then it's out, smartass." Val sauntered over to Hunter, her smoky eyeliner-rimmed eyes appraising him again. "Stand up," she said. "Up, up."

Hunter pushed off the stool, and the look he gave me was full of *is this bitch for real?* Yes. Yes, she was.

"Now turn," Val said, indicating for him to circle around so she could inspect him from all angles. Hunter sighed but did it anyway, probably of the same thought process I was—just get her the hell out already.

"Hmm. On second thought… I'll be willing to forgive the eyesore in the shop if I can trade it for the eye candy standing in front of me." Pursing her lips, she nodded, and then looked back at me. "Dress this little beefcake up in something that screams 'God of a million instantaneous orgasms,' and make sure he's here by seven." She reached past Hunter, grabbed the cherry off the top of his sundae, and popped it into her mouth before giving him one last look. Then she sashayed to the door, which I gladly held open for her, and as she walked by me, she said, "And make sure to stock extra cream."

Chapter Eight
Matchmaker, Matchmaker, Make Me a Match

"ALL RIGHT, EVERYBODY, I need cocks on one side, pussycats on the other. Chop chop, now, or I'll make you all play strip Simon Says." Val stood at the front of Licked the next evening, dressed in an elegant crimson dress that looked out of place with the words spewing out of her mouth as she commanded the room.

The men and women gathered for the mixer HLS—Hook, Line, and Sinker Matchmaking Company—was holding scattered to the far sides of the room like worker bees for Queen Val. And weren't they the cream of the crop: the men donned suits and ties; the women wore extravagant cocktail dresses and sky-high heels that had me lusting with some serious shoe envy.

For my part, I stayed behind the bar with Amber,

who was helping with the drinks since my usual wingwoman, Zoe, was out. Unlike other matchmaking companies, Val didn't throw down a two-drink rule, which made it a more-than-profitable night for me. In addition to the variety of mixed drinks, the special tonight was a First Base boozy shake. Guaranteed to help *some* get lucky tonight. Hey, I do my part.

I was telling myself not to watch the door. Not to notice that a certain someone hadn't showed up after all, which I would certainly hear no end of from Val later. Hunter probably didn't own anything fit for tonight's dress code, since he lived in jeans and t-shirts. But I wasn't thinking about that—much.

Focusing my attention back on the drink I was making, I added an extra cherry and slid it across the bar to an attractive forty-something guy who winked at me as he paid.

Dude. I just put a cherry in your drink. You're not screaming overly masculine and sexy. I mean, he could've gone with Cognac.

"Miss? Could I get a Cosmopolitan?"

I shook my head and pointed at the specials on the counter sign. "If you're looking for fruity, the Red-Headed Slut is probably up your alley."

The blond let out an exaggerated sigh and inspected her manicured nails. "Could you manage Grey Goose, because I only do top-shelf. Thanks."

She turned her back toward me before I could

explain that it was Jäger and not vodka in the drink. Whatever. She'd never know the difference.

I caught Shayne looking at me and quickly rolling her eyes from where she was planted next to Val, and I smothered a laugh. We didn't have to say anything, and we knew—bitches were crazy.

Val clapped loudly to get everyone's attention. "So the first thing we're going to do this evening is—"

The jingle of someone entering the front door had Val's mouth opening and eyes narrowing like she was about to give a lecture, but when she turned around, all that came out was, "You're late."

As the handsome man came into view, it took me a moment to realize who it was, and when recognition dawned, my jaw dropped. With his hair styled back instead of flopping across his forehead, and wearing a tailored black suit and tie, Hunter was…

Well, hell. He was kind of breathtaking, wasn't he?

His eyes found mine, and his lips lifted in greeting. I forced myself to close my mouth.

As he moved past Val toward the bar, she grabbed the crook of his arm. "Where do you think you're going, fancy pants? Move your hot ass over to the right. You can get a drink later."

I was shocked to see Hunter without a smartass retort, and even more shocked when he did what she said. As he leaned against the wall with about twenty-five other guys, he crossed his arms and smirked at me.

What the hell does that look mean?

"Excuse me, could you please add some whipped cream? It tastes too liquory." The blond was back, pushing her Red-Headed Slut my way. Considering the contents of the glass were about half gone, I doubted she'd had to force it down. Whipped cream wasn't an ingredient in the drink, but I added a couple swirls anyway. She probably wouldn't be getting any other cream later with that attitude. Wink wink.

Val had split the men and women into groups of six, three of each sex, and was walking through the room observing and popping in to make conversation until the alcohol hit and the shyness went away.

Shayne sighed as she leaned her hip on the bar. "That guy in the suspenders has already groped my arse twice. When I complained to Val, she told me he was probably just perfecting his squeeze for later." She cut her eyes at me. "I should've told him to go play with hers, but he'd need four hands and gloves."

I picked up the shot glass of her favorite, Rattlesnake, from under the bar that I'd poured a few minutes ago for when she got a break, and passed it to her. "I don't know how you work with her. Or why. I'm convinced you're a saint."

"Glutton for punishment, more like." She brushed a strand of her long, fiery red curls behind her ear, looked in Val's direction, and then shot the 'snake. Poor thing.

Though Shayne was a more successful matchmaker

than Val, and the true brains behind the operation, she was under the assumption she needed Val more than Val needed her. Which was the furthest thing from the truth. If you asked me, Shayne was terrified of branching out on her own. Oh, she seemed confident, what with her sweet Aussie charm and her ability to put together a couple out of the most odd pairing, but I knew the truth. And the truth was that she'd rather deal with Val and stay in her comfort zone than take a flying leap off a cliff and start her own business.

Hah. Like I did. *And look at the mess I'm making,* I thought, glancing at the tarp.

Shayne nodded at the group by the jukebox as she popped a mint in her mouth. "Isn't that your builder?"

When I looked over to whom she was referring to, I caught Hunter staring at me, and I quickly looked away again. "He's not *my* builder."

"You know what I mean. What's he doing here? He wasn't on my list for the mixer."

"Val orgasmed when she stopped by yesterday to complain about the renovations and saw him." I shrugged. "Even trade."

"Huh." Shayne didn't bother asking for more details about what that visit had entailed. She could probably guess them by now. "Cleans up well, doesn't he?"

Nope. Wasn't touching that. I was keeping my lips shut. If I didn't, I'd launch into how good he looked when he was dirty, and then that would have me thinking of other ways he could get dirty—

"Ry?" Shayne asked.

"Yeah?"

"I said how's Cameron?"

Yeah, Cameron—the guy you're crazy about. "Cameron…he's good, I think. I got a message from him saying he'd made it to Hong Kong, so I'm sure he's having a blast."

"Uh huh." Shayne raised an eyebrow before turning back to check Val's status. She was draped all over two of the male clients, and they looked appropriately horrified. "Oh what the hell is she…fuck me, I'll be back."

The next half-hour passed in a blur, making drinks and tending to Val's nagging requests: Could we change the music to something not so old-fashioned? I'm sweating like a whore in church, could you turn the air down? Way down? One thing I was actively *not* doing, though, was keeping tabs on Hunter. He'd been hopping from group to group, Shayne having organized the whole thing like a round of standing musical chairs. He was currently in a circle that included the annoying blond I'd waited on earlier, and to say she had goo-goo eyes for Hunter was an understatement. Actually, it looked like the other two girls standing by her did as well.

I looked him over with a more critical eye. I guessed I could see the appeal if you liked the ruggedly handsome type. The way he was giving each person one-on-one attention as if they were the only ones in the room could also be seen as a plus, I supposed. He wasn't as tall as Cameron, but he still commanded attention, but probably because he was so bossy. The way he took control of every situation and handled it might be something other women would like. *But not me.*

The blond bimbo laughed at something Hunter said, giving her an excuse to lay her hand on his arm. I stared daggers at her ugly orange fake nails. Who wore orange outside of October, anyway?

Rolling my eyes, I made myself look away and grabbed the almost-empty container of whipped cream and took it to the kitchen. After pulling out the new batch I'd made this morning, I went back out to the front and stopped when I saw Hunter standing at the bar. I gave him a tight-lipped smile before putting the container in the fridge.

"How's date night going?" I asked.

"Best night of my life," he said with a smirk. Up close I could smell the faint hint of whatever sex-in-a-bottle cologne he was wearing. That had to be it. Pheromone cologne, making all the girls stop and drool. Cheater.

I nodded at the women behind him who were stealing glances to make sure he was coming back. "Looks like you've got an adoring fan club already. You must not have opened your mouth yet."

His grin grew wider. "They don't leave a lot of room to say much. But that's the trick. Let the woman talk, and you come off as a great listener."

"Ah, spoken like a true playboy."

"Is that how you see me?"

Shrugging, I said, "I don't really notice one way or another."

"I saw your reaction when I walked in. Didn't think I owned anything fancier than jeans and t-shirts?"

"Was just surprised to see you here, that's all. Didn't think this was your kind of thing."

"It's not." Hunter shook his head. "I just thought after meeting that crazy woman in charge maybe you wouldn't want to face the love fest alone."

"I'm doing just fine, but thanks."

"Yeah, I can see that." He looked as though he wanted to say something else but stopped himself.

Well of course he wanted something else—I hadn't even offered him a drink.

"Sorry, can I get you something?"

He leaned over the counter like he was going to tell me a secret. "I'd love whatever your friend took a shot of earlier." Looking back over his shoulder at the hungry women still eyeing him, he said, "Make that two."

I poured him two shots of the Rattlesnake concoction, and then made him an alcoholic Shirley Temple chaser, heavy on the grenadine so it turned bright pink. Then I topped it off with a straw and a purple umbrella. His brows were knitted as he took the drink out of my hands.

"You're too kind," he said, holding the glass as if there were some sort of growth coming out of it.

"Try it. You'll like it. And besides." I leaned over the counter like he'd done a minute ago. "Women love a man who wears pink."

There was a fire in Hunter's eyes when I pulled away. His lips wrapped around the bendy straw I'd stuck inside the drink for an amusing effect, but as he sucked the juice into his mouth, there was nothing funny about it.

No, funny was not the right word. Figures he could make tasting a girly cocktail look sexy as hell. My face was getting warmer, and Hunter must've noticed, because his lips left the straw and he grinned again.

"I do love it pink and juicy." He backed away as my eyes grew bigger, and I threw my towel in his direction. Laughing, he turned away and rejoined his group, the women gladly welcoming him back to the fold.

Cocky shit. Next time I was spiking his drink with Drano.

IT HAD TAKEN Shayne and me a good half-hour to kick out the last of the stragglers—and that included Hunter, who'd insisted on helping move the tables and chairs back in order. I couldn't complain too much, though, because after a long day I was dead on my feet.

As I untied my apron, a buzzing in the front pocket had me jumping. When I pulled out my cell, the screen showed Cameron was calling, and I couldn't help the smile that spread across my face. After turning out the lights in the shop and opening the door that led to my apartment, I hit the answer button. "Cameron."

"Hey, I caught you. It's not a bad time, is it?"

Making my way up the stairs, I pulled the phone away from my ear to glance at the time. Almost midnight, which meant it was—I counted on my fingers—about three p.m. or so there. "Not at all. Just closing up shop. How's everything going over there?"

"Eh, could be better. Negotiations have been a bit intense and things are running behind schedule, so I apologize for not calling sooner."

"That's okay. It's been crazy here too."

"Hunter taking care of you?"

I froze. *Uh…no, of course not. I mean…not like that.*

A burst of static came through the phone and then I heard, "Can't get a decent connection here to save my life. You there?"

Swallowing, I said, "Yeah. Yeah, I'm here."

"I asked how the construction is coming along."

Ohhhh that. Right. Of course that was what he meant by Hunter taking care of me. I mean, what else would it be?

"Going great so far, except for the furniture order the other contractor decided not to put in," I said. "But Hunter told me about a specialty place near Palm Desert that can do custom designs in the time frame I need them. My fingers are crossed that they'll turn out better than the ones I'd settled on originally."

"Oh yeah, Mitch is great, but damn that last guy was

a nightmare. I'm glad Hunter's got everything under control. I knew he would."

Yeah, control is definitely the word that springs to mind when I think of that guy.

"So when are you coming back?" I asked.

A heavy sigh came through the phone. "I was supposed to be back by the weekend, but the way things are going, it looks like I'll have to be here a little longer."

Well, dammit. I was glad he couldn't see my frown through the phone. Flicking on a lamp in my living room, I said, "I've heard the food there is interesting."

"That's an understatement. I had chicken feet the other day. Looked crazy but didn't taste too bad. Crunchy."

Wrinkling my nose, I said, "I think I'd have to pass on that one."

"I bet I could get you to try it. There's also something called snake soup we could check out." I could picture the smile on his face as he said it, so sure I'd be up for an adventurous food tasting. But no. Hell no. Despite my wild sense of style, my palate for anything *not* a dessert was actually a little...well, vanilla.

"I think I'd rather live vicariously through you." I kicked my shoes off into the closet and then collapsed onto my bed.

"You sound tired."

"It's been a bit of a long day. Had a matchmaking event tonight that ran a bit late. Your buddy was there."

There was a pause. "Are you talking about Hunter?"

"Yeah."

"He was there? At a matchmaking thing?" He sounded skeptical.

"Is that surprising? Seems like another way to meet women, right?"

"Uh…yeah, I guess so. Hang on one sec." Cameron's voice became muffled, but I could hear him speaking with someone and then a door shut. "Sorry, my three thirty is here early, but I'll call you soon?"

"Looking forward to it."

"Oh, and uh…don't *you* go to one of those matchmaker things. Please."

Please. Hanging up with a huge smile on my face, I stretched out on the bed. He didn't want me to date anyone, did he? Well, since he'd asked so nicely…

"THERE'S A REASON you have that walking orgasm in a creamery called Licked, right?" Paige was chewing on the end of her straw as she sat on the edge of the barstool Wednesday afternoon, her gaze on Hunter, who was clearly outlined through the clear tarp. "I mean…fuck me, please."

"Tell me about it," Shayne said. "I've gained five pounds this week from coming to watch him nail that wood with his thick hammer."

I rolled my eyes. "Oh my G—"

Paige held up her hand. "Admit it. You may be crazy about his friend or whatever, but you can't tell me he's not drool-worthy. I will seriously question our friendship *and* your eyesight."

Ignoring her, I smiled at the customers who'd just walked in and took their order, even though they seemed to be more interested in what every other woman in the shop had their eyes on.

It was week two of Hunter's crew at the After Dark, and the daytime crowd was becoming noticeably larger. And predominately women, who all wanted a view of the so-called walking orgasm next door. I'd considered putting back up that hideous black tarp, but business was business, and if offering sweaty construction guys as a way to kick up sales was working, I was not about to complain. Much.

When I was finished making their sundaes, I headed back to the girls, who had been taking extended lunch breaks this week just to come visit my little shop. Hah.

"Shayne, what's the word after the mixer the other night?" I asked.

She groaned. "Apparently Val went home with the two guys she was draped over all evening. It's a wonder we even have male clients with the way she buggers around. And get this, she set me up with this skeez-o next week, which she says isn't a date. It's a 'client meeting.'"

"That seems to happen a lot with her," I said.

"I can't tell if she's using me to bring in big-name clients, or if she just wants me married off because an office of single matchmakers isn't good business."

"And being a matchmaker with a reputation for being a psychotic slutbag pill-popper *is* good business?" Paige asked. "Tell her to fuck right off."

I retied my loosened apron strings. "Hey, have you guys seen Quinn this week? She hasn't returned my messages."

"She told me she had to jet and would be back Sunday." Paige shrugged. "Don't ask me where. One of these days, we need to tie her down and force her to admit she's really a KGB operative."

"You know," I said, "I heard her speak in a language that sounded like Russian on the phone once, so that's entirely plausible."

"I knew it."

"Speaking of out of town," Shayne said, "what's the latest on Cameron?"

A grin spread across my face. "He's called and messaged a few times. The time difference makes it hard to have a conversation, since it's usually seven a.m. when he calls, but we're talking. I'll see him when he gets back."

"Any idea when that will be?"

"Not really. Work is taking a little longer than he expected, so…" I shrugged.

"Well, what about…" Shayne paused, and then said, "You know. The good stuff."

"The good stuff? What are you talking about?" I asked.

"Phone sex," Paige said, and then took out her straw to lick off the whipped cream.

"Excuse me? I can't have phone sex with him. We haven't even kissed yet." I shook my head. "You've lost your mind."

"The guy is in Hong Kong, where he could be taking advantage of the five-dollar prostitutes on every corner. Give him a little something to tide him over and have him dying to come back and straight into your bed. This is a no-brainer."

Shayne twisted her lips and shrugged. "She does have a point."

"How would I even… I mean, how do you even bring that up?"

"Just call him and say hey, I'm touching myself, now take your pants off," Paige said, and then her gaze darted between Shayne and me. "What? That's what I'd do."

"Oh my God, would you keep your voice down," I said, looking around to make sure no one was paying attention. I shouldn't have worried, though, because they were otherwise occupied by watching my hired Chippendale workers.

Paige pushed her empty glass toward me. "I'm telling you. You need to give him something to look forward to when he gets back. Sex it up. Trust me, he's not gonna say no."

"And if he doesn't go for it?" I asked.

Shayne nodded next door. "Then I would jump all over that *quick hot*."

"I am so gonna need a lot of alcohol for this," I muttered.

"And that," Paige said with a big smile, "can be

easily arranged. Zoe's closing tonight, right?"

"Yes..."

"The new Boca Lounge is opening downtown. Let's get you smashed."

PAIGE HAD DONE her friendly duty and handed me more shots than I could remember doing in a long time, so I had enough liquid courage in me now to probably attack Cameron in person if he'd been around.

After kicking off my heels, I flopped onto my bed, the room spinning slightly. If I was going to do this, it would have to be now, otherwise the night was a waste and I'd pass out in two minutes flat.

Reaching over, I grabbed my cell off the nightstand and scrolled to Cameron's number. Hitting the call button, I sat up and leaned back against my headboard as I waited to see if he'd answer.

Two rings, and then, "Ryleigh?"

"That would be me," I said with a hiccup. Covering my mouth, I waited to make sure another one wasn't coming before saying, "Are you busy?" I hoped the answer was no, but I couldn't remember what time it was there, and I wasn't about to count on my fingers to figure it out.

"I just got back to the hotel to grab a few things before our dinner meeting."

"So you're in your hotel…alone?" I asked.

"I am."

"And what are you doing aaaaall alone?"

I could hear the amusement in his voice when he said, "Nothing that can't wait. Is there something I can help you with, Miss Phillips?"

"I wish you were here," I said, the alcohol pushing me out of my comfort zone.

"Oh yeah? You want to take advantage of me?"

"Mhmm." I scooted down the bed until I was lying flat on my back. "Or maybe you could take advantage of me." Even though I could hear the words coming out of my mouth, I couldn't believe I was actually saying them. Damn those chocolate cake shots.

"Where are you right now?"

"On my bed. You wanna join me?"

His voice was husky when he answered, "I'm on my way."

I sighed. "Tease."

"I won't be teasing when I get back and we pick up where we left off."

A shiver ran through me, and I ran my hand over my stomach. "I'd like that. Maybe we could play now?"

I heard the background noise fall silent, as though he'd turned off the television, and then he was back. "Are you still in one of those sexy dresses you always wear?"

"For the moment. Is there something else you'd prefer?"

"No, stay just like that. I'd want to pull it off you myself."

Oh hell yes.

"You should do that," I said. "You should definitely do that."

When I closed my eyes, I imagined Cameron's face hovering above me, his fingers trailing down my neck, between my breasts, over my stomach, and then lower…

"I want to touch you," he said, and I moaned.

"I want that too." My voice came out breathy, and I moved my fingers lower, pretending it was his warm, rough fingers reaching down to cover my—

My eyes flew open and I moved my hand away. Fuck. Those were not Cameron's fingers I'd been thinking of.

"Where's your hand, Ryleigh?"

My hand was…not where he wanted it to be. Dammit, why was his stupid roommate invading our attempt at phone sex?

Mentally flicking off Hunter, I ran my fingers between my thighs and called to mind Cameron's face once more. Only I couldn't find it. It was like his file had been replaced with a gorgeous, but right now pain-in-the-ass, dark-headed man that had no right to be there.

Images flipped through my mind like a carousel: Hunter's grin when he caught me watching him at the mixer, the way his hair flopped over his forehead as he concentrated. I tried to shut him out, but he was like a fungus—he just kept fucking growing.

"Ryleigh?" Cameron said. "Did you fall asleep?"

I was gonna kick my own ass for this tomorrow. Or in about one minute. Holding up the covers to the receiver, I ran it across so that it hopefully sounded like static on his end, and said, "Sorry…bad…connection…we'll try…again," before hitting the end button.

"Ugh." I threw my phone across the room and kicked my legs, tantrum style, not believing I'd just ended what should've been a hot night with Cameron because I couldn't stop visualizing someone I definitely did *not* want. Someone who purposely went out of his way to antagonize me. Someone getting in the way of hot phone sex with my dream guy.

"Screw off, Hunter Morgan," I said in the empty room. "Screw the hell off."

YOU ARE AN idiot of the highest order, I told myself for the tenth time in the last hour. It was Saturday night, and as I stood on the doorstep of the last place I expected to be, I debated whether to knock. Maybe I could tell him something came up at the shop and we'd have to discuss things tomorrow, or that I hit an old lady with my car and had to spend the night in the ER waiting room.

No. Bad karma.

With my arms crossed tightly over my chest, I chewed on my lip and debated my other options. I could knock and go inside, and then…well, we'd work like we'd discussed at the shop today. And then I'd go home. And that would be that.

But something about that option had me jittery as

hell. I'd been staring at the black door with the numbers 986 in silver for at least five minutes, and soon the neighbors would probably start peeking out of their blinds.

No. This was a bad idea. Turning on my heel, I went back to my car. Yes, this was a very bad id—

"Ryleigh?"

Shit.

Pivoting slowly, I gave a halfhearted wave. "Hey, Hunter."

"Not leaving, are you?" he asked.

Busted. I headed back up the sidewalk. "No, I was just…going to get something out of my car."

"Ah, okay. I'll wait."

"You'll wait…" I said, and then shook my head. "Nah, it's not important."

"You sure?" he asked.

"Positive."

He held the front door open for me to pass, but didn't move, which meant I had to brush against him to get inside. I could feel the heat of his body through his shirt, but I wasn't about to stop and linger.

Damn, damn, damn, this was so not good.

I walked in to see the blueprints laid out across the circular oak table in the dining area. So I *was* here to work. Well, that was a relief. He wasn't going to tear my clothes off after all.

"Can I get you a drink?" Hunter asked, grabbing two wine glasses that hung from a rack in the kitchen. There was no way in hell I was drinking with him here on his turf. *His and Cameron's turf,* I reminded myself.

When I shook my head, he frowned and then put the extra glass back. "Suit yourself."

"I never pictured you for a wine guy," I said when he sat down across from me at the table and set his glass of red down.

"What does a wine guy look like?"

"Suave and debonair, maybe a sophisticated businessman—"

"Like Cameron." Hunter's jaw ticked.

"Well…yeah."

"He hates wine."

"Oh."

He took a long gulp of the ruby liquid. "So what do I look like, then? Wait, let me guess," he said, his eyes narrowing slightly. "Bud Light or PBRs, right?"

"I would've said maybe Corona. Or rum and Coke."

Hunter shook his head. "And what is it the boozy shake queen likes? Other than ice cream with her alcohol."

"It's the best of both worlds, which you'd know if you tried one."

"I might just have to do that," he said. "Can't hurt to have a taste."

As the glass went to his lips again, I swallowed hard. Maybe letting him have a taste wouldn't be such a great idea. He'd probably become addicted, and then I'd never get rid of him.

Of course, my brain wasn't just thinking about the boozy shakes then.

Returning my focus to the plans laid out on the table, I cleared my throat. "So you said there needed to be changes. You mean incredibly minor ones that won't be any issue at all, right?"

"Mhmm. Practically nonexistent."

"Then let's get started."

"We'll have to make the bar a few inches longer to accommodate the plumbing."

"And?"

Hunter scanned the plans and then shrugged. "That's it."

I gaped at him. "That's it? I came all this way for a few measly inches?"

When he burst into laughter, I flushed, realizing how he took it. I didn't mean *those* inches.

With a growl, I said, "You could've gone over these things with me in the shop."

"You're right, I could've. I had an ulterior motive."

My heart thumped in my chest. Okay, so he was a little bolder than I thought. It was time to have my Louboutin Summerissima sandals hauling ass out the door.

"Look, I don't know what you thought—"

Hunter stood up. "Just wait here," he said, then threw back the rest of his wine before disappearing into his bedroom. If he came back out with a box of Trojans, my knee was going to make sure he didn't have an appendage left to use them on.

When he returned, there was a stack of what looked like scrapbooks in his arms, and he dropped them on the table in front of me with a loud thump.

My brow knitted in confusion. "What's this?"

"Designs to look through before we meet with Mitch."

"But I already have ideas in mind. The ones that should've been ordered."

"And those were fine, but I have a feeling you want something a little more…you."

"Those are me."

Hunter cocked his head to the side. "Would you just look at them?"

With a sigh, I opened the book on top of the pile and flipped to the first page. My eyes widened at the array of lacquered black stools with magenta cushioned seats. They were even set against white and black checkered tile flooring, just like the kind in my shop. The effect was visually stunning.

"I thought you might like those," Hunter said, a smile creeping onto his lips.

I wasn't about to let him have the satisfaction of being right. *Hell no.* "They're not bad."

"Not bad? Your eyes just popped out of your head."

Flipping the page, I saw more barstools, this time in a mirage of some of my favorite colors—aqua, yellow, and amethyst. Totally up my alley. The next page had funky tables and booths; the next had different designs for the high-top tables and chairs. All bold. All eclectic. All me.

When I looked up, Hunter was watching me. "Where did you find this stuff?" I asked.

"Do you like it?"

Dammit. I did not want to admit defeat, but the truth was that these pieces blew mine out of the water and made them look plain in comparison. Blowing out a breath, I said, "Fine. Yes. They're amazing."

Hunter gave me a dazzling grin, stood up, and grabbed his glass. "Look at the book underneath that one. It's got some great ideas for lighting."

As I was flipping through that one and oohing and ahhing over everything, Hunter came back with a full wine glass…and one for me.

"Tell me you don't like it," he said when he caught my disapproving look.

"I don't like it."

"Try it and then tell me."

"You're rather pushy, you know that, right?"

"Maybe I know what you'd like."

"Maybe you don't know me at all."

As I glared at him across the table, he stared right back. "I haven't been too far off base with anything yet."

And dammit, he was right. I hated that he was right. I wasn't even sure why I wanted to prove him wrong, but since I wasn't a huge red wine fan, I'd do it now. Picking up the glass, I held it up in a mock salute, and then took a small sip. The instant the flavors of blackberry, chocolate, and vanilla landed on my tongue, I knew I'd lost this round.

"For fuck's sake," I muttered, while Hunter gave a victory smile. "I don't even like red."

"Don't worry, I won't tell anyone."

"I wonder what I could pair this with for a shake…I could call it the Red Devil." I looked pointedly at him.

His hand went over his heart. "I'd be honored."

I shook my head and took another sip before pointing at the lighting on the page. "Could we do something like this but have it shine through the bar? So you can see the lights underneath?"

Hunter's brow went up. "You mean a clear bar?"

"Well…yeah. Or maybe not clear, more, um…foggy? Is that the word?"

"Frosted."

"Yeah, frosted."

Hunter turned the book to face him and flipped to the next page. "Like this?"

"I'll be damned. Exactly like that. Is that feasible?"

Hunter's eyes flicked up to mine. "Anything you want."

His gaze had my stomach flipping, and I couldn't force any words out of my mouth. Not even a wise-ass comeback. All I could do was pry my eyes away from his.

"Let's nail down a few that you like, and when we see Mitch, he'll let you know what's doable in the time frame and in your budget," he said. "Sound good?"

I nodded.

"We're still on for Monday morning, right? I'll pick you up at ten."

That had my voice coming back. "There's no need to do that. I can drive myself."

"It's three hours away. It's stupid to take two cars."

Okay, that *was* a little ridiculous. I tried to think of another reason not to be alone in the car with him for a long period of time.

"I've got a truck, and we might be coming back with a few pieces, so it makes sense for me to drive. Any other arguments?"

I sighed.

"Good."

"Is there anything else we need to go over?" I asked. There was no way I was coming back for a return trip. Better knock it all out at once.

"I guess not." He gestured to the books. "Feel free to take whatever you want and look over them."

"Yeah, I'll do that," I said, placing the two I'd already gone through in a separate pile so I could go through the others. "I'll give them back to you on—shit."

My hand knocked into my glass and it tumbled over, the wine splattering onto my lap. Against my white dress, the red liquid resembled something out of a murder scene.

"Don't move." Hunter leaped up and grabbed a roll of paper towels and a plastic bag before kneeling in front of me. My hands were holding the edges of my dress up so the contents wouldn't get all over the floor. He began to wipe at the mess in my lap, discarding the towels into the bag as they each soaked up the wine.

"I'm so sorry. That's a huge reason not to drink red wine. Or to wear white, I suppose," I said. Yeah, white anything wasn't the smartest idea, and this dress would be going in the trash tonight for sure.

"Nah, it all comes off," he said, his hands pressing down on my thighs, and it was then that it occurred to me where he was touching me. He ripped off another paper towel and pressed down where my hip met my thigh. And again and again until the towel soaked and he had to get another. I just sat there, letting him do it, studying the lines of his face as he cleaned me off.

His skin was so tan compared to mine, and I wondered if it was his natural tone or from hours spent at the beach. His hair fell onto his forehead, and I ached to push it back and thread my fingers through the thick strands. This time, he pressed down a few inches to the left, right in the center where my—

I pushed his hands away, feeling breathless. He looked up in confusion, and I swallowed. "I can do it," I whispered.

He looked down at where he'd been touching me, and it seemed to dawn on him then where his hands had been. Without a word, he handed me the roll of paper towels and got up off the floor. Then he wiped away the drops from the table and took my empty glass to the kitchen.

Letting out a shaky breath, I finished cleaning my dress as best I could, and then handed him the bag to throw away.

My knees wobbled as I got to my feet, and I was thankful his back was turned. The door to Cameron's room was cracked, and I could see the impeccably made bed, the spotless floors and dressers. He seemed to be as put together as he looked. *Unlike me,* I thought as I looked down at my ruined dress.

Here I was, in his apartment, having drinks and trying not to ogle his best friend and roommate. *What the hell is wrong with me?*

A burst of longing ripped through my chest. I wished he were there. He suddenly felt like a safety blanket, something familiar and steady. Maybe I should call him… Glancing at the wall clock, I added fifteen hours. It would be midafternoon there now. Yes, good plan. Now I just needed to get the hell out of here before the tension suffocated me.

"I'll carry them," Hunter said when I reached for the design books. I didn't bother putting up a complaint, seeing as my arms still felt like Jell-O. The effect he had on me was lingering, and I didn't like that a damn bit.

He seemed to sense my mood and stayed quiet as he followed me to my car. After putting the books on the floor of the backseat, he rested his hand on the door. Running his fingers through his hair, he sighed, and then said, "Ryleigh, I—"

"I need to get going," I interrupted. "Thank you for

the books. I'll keep them somewhere safe." I quickly slid into the driver's seat before he could say any more. Though I wouldn't meet his eyes, I knew he was staring at me.

After a long moment, he let out a heavy breath and shut the back door. "Drive safe."

Nodding, I put the car in gear and didn't bother looking his way before flying down the street.

What was Hunter playing at? He knew I was interested in Cameron, yet everything in me was screaming warnings that the guy was looking to make his move. Unless I was reading the signs wrong, and I didn't think I was.

Hunter wasn't giving up until, true to his name, he'd successfully hunted and captured his prey.

His prey being…me.

Chapter Eleven

Trail of Broken Hearts

MY STOMACH HAD been in knots for over twenty-four hours. Hunter would be picking me up any minute, and I was struggling not to bite off every one of my nails while I waited. After leaving his house Saturday night, I'd been restless, half tempted to call off the trip and invest in plastic chairs and cups.

Maybe I was reading too much into this. He was a flirty guy, yeah, but he hadn't actually *tried* anything with me. I bet he did that with all the girls. A few hours in the car would be no big deal. I'd even brought a pair of headphones and stashed them in my purse in case of an emergency—like listening to country music.

Hunter's black truck pulled into a space in front of the shop, and he jumped out, dressed casually in jeans and a white shirt. He looked freshly showered…and utterly delicious.

He opened the passenger's-side door for me and grinned. "Mornin', sunshine."

I tried for a smile. "Good morning."

"You know, for someone who's about to go shopping, I thought you'd be more excited."

Hoping he wouldn't see right through me, I slid onto the seat and said, "Maybe we can stop for some caffeine?"

"I thought you might say that," Hunter said when he'd gotten in the truck. He pulled a coffee cup out of the center console and handed it to me before sipping out of his own.

"Pickup service *and* coffee. I could get used to that." As soon as the words were out of my mouth, I wanted to take them back. I didn't mean I could get used to *him* picking me up and getting me coffee every day, because that would imply something I was *not* thinking about. I had just meant in general. Of course.

Luckily, he didn't comment, just gave me a half-smile and pulled out onto the road.

I took a sip, and wouldn't you know it—the coffee was delicious, just like the man who'd made it. But he'd added some kind of sweetener I couldn't pinpoint.

"What did you put in this?" I asked.

"Can't tell you that."

"Why? Some kind of secret recipe?"

"Special recipe, yes."

"Like…?"

He glanced at me out of the corner of his eye. "You can call it Hunter's sweet cream—ow." Hunter rubbed his arm where I'd punched him. "What? You asked."

"Is it possible for you to stay PG during this trip?"

"I don't know, is it possible you could keep your hands to yourself, Tyson?"

"Yes."

"Then maybe."

I sighed and drank my coffee in silence as he pulled onto the freeway. He looked like a car model with his hand lying on top of the steering wheel and the other on the gear shift, his shaggy brown hair whipping across his forehead from the wind that was blowing in through the cracked windows. My hair was up and not going anywhere, so I didn't mind the fresh air. I also didn't mind that he hadn't bothered to turn the radio on either, in case his preference really *was* country music.

The twisted ball of trepidation in my stomach eased the farther we drove away from L.A.

See? This wasn't so bad. I could be in a car with him and be platonic. It wasn't like I was visualizing what he looked like naked. Wait…dammit, why did I just think of that?

Don't visualize him naked, don't visualize him naked. Subject change…

"Oh, by the way," I said, "I brought a couple of the books you gave me to look through so I could show Mitch.

Remind me to give you the rest when we get back." *Yes, good. Focus on work stuff.*

"Find anything you like?"

"Actually, it was hard to find anything not to be totally obsessed with. I might need help narrowing it down."

"That's what today is for."

I picked at the sleeve of the coffee cup. "I don't remember if I said thank you for this. And if I did, thank you again. I thought I had all my ducks in a row a long time ago."

"Everything happens for a reason, right?"

"I could've done without the shady builder stress, but I suppose you're right."

"A better way to look at it would be to say you completely lucked out by snagging me."

Rolling my eyes, I said, "So modest."

"Say it. 'Hunter, I'm so lucky you walked through my door.'"

"I am *not* saying that."

"You better say it. Don't make me turn this truck around. Your guests will be drinking those boozy shakes of yours while sitting Indian style on the cold, hard floor."

"I already said thank you."

"Ryleigh..." he said with a growl.

Wow... My name sounded pretty hot like that—

Wait, no, no, no. Don't even go there.

"Fine. I'm the luckiest person in the whole world that

Hunter Morgan strolled into my little shop and begged to take over from shitty contractors."

"You forgot to say how hot you think that Hunter Morgan is."

"You're ridiculous," I muttered.

His grin grew wider. "Thank you."

"So please tell me how you got to be the best construction worker ever in the world."

"Second best. My old man's the first. Has his own business just outside of Chicago and had me and my brothers building cabinets when we were eight."

I twisted in my seat to face him. "Wait, you're from Chicago?"

"Born and raised."

"You don't sound like it. Well, maybe you have a little bit of an accent, now that you mention it."

"Means I've been here too long."

"My friend Shayne is from Australia and still sounds like it."

"I bet her friends back in Oz would beg to differ."

"True. So what brought you to L.A. in the first place?"

A sad smile twisted his lips. "Followed a girl."

"Aw, you little sap. What happened? Did she break your heart?"

"How do you know I didn't do the heartbreaking?"

"Because you wouldn't still be here. I bet you stayed, licking your wounds and trying to win her back. And then before you knew it, you had life and friends here and going back to Chicago meant starting over."

He looked over at me before focusing back on the road. "Seems like you've got me figured out."

"Am I close?"

"You're right about one thing," he said. "I did stay here."

"That's it?"

"Just about."

"You're not good at this whole getting to know you, making conversation thing."

"What else did you want to know?"

What *else*… I guessed that was his way of shutting down *that* topic. I was curious about how he'd met Cameron, why they lived together when it was obvious they both did well in their respective businesses, but I didn't feel right bringing Cameron up. Silly, since there was nothing going on between Hunter and me, but still.

"You said brothers. How many do you have?" I asked.

"Three. And a sister."

"Damn. Midwesterners like to breed, huh?"

Hunter choked on his coffee, and when he looked my way, I gave him a mischievous grin.

We talked about his siblings…the fact that I was an only child…my grandparents' ice cream shop where I'd spent my summers and developed "mad ice creamery skills," as he called them, and before I knew it, three hours had flown by and we were passing the city of Palm Desert.

"Are you sure you're going the right way?" I asked as he continued driving farther to what looked like a whole lot of Boonyville to me. We were surrounded by…well, nothing. We seemed to be going in the opposite direction of town.

"Patience is a virtue," he said, easing the car onto a dirt road that seemed to have popped up out of nowhere.

I turned my body so that I was leaning against the door. "You're taking me somewhere to chop me into tiny pieces, aren't you?"

"It was supposed to be a surprise," Hunter said, keeping a straight face.

"You could've at least let me pick out my best dress for the occasion."

"You look grea—" He caught himself and shrugged. "You'll do."

Was he about to say that I looked great? *Whoa.* That shouldn't have made me bite down on my lip to keep from smiling, but I did. Dammit.

Hunter turned left again, and as we drove up the dusty trail, the Garden of Eden came into view. At least that was what it looked like to me.

"Are you serious?" I said, scooting to the edge of my seat, my mouth falling open. "Is this where we're going?"

"This is your final resting place, yes."

"Wow."

It was like a tropical rainforest had been dropped in

the middle of the desert. Palm trees stood at attention overlooking the lush greenery surrounding the adobe property. Flowers of every color lined the pathway, as did the elaborate fountain and the antique swing off to the side in the middle of the garden. The mixture of new and old shouldn't have made sense, but somehow it worked.

Yeah. This was so up my alley.

When we got out of the car, a robust man in a Hawaiian shirt was coming down the front steps to greet us. His jet-black hair trailed down his back, glistening in the sun. It was enough to bring on a serious case of hair lust.

"About time you came back around," he said to Hunter, pulling him in for a hug and clapping him on the back. "Been too long. Molly was beginning to think you were never coming back."

"Molly? Forgetting your girlfriends already?" I asked Hunter.

As if on cue, a giant Great Dane loped down the stairs and made a beeline for Hunter, jumping on him so its paws were on his chest. Hunter laughed as his face was smothered in wet kisses. "I missed you too, girl."

"Molly, get down," the man said, before shaking his head. He gave me an apologetic smile. "Mitch," he said, shaking my hand. "You must be Ryleigh. Hunter tells me you've got a great little ice creamery in the city."

"Nice to meet you. And thank you. I'm a little biased, but I think it's pretty nice."

"Well, come on in, I know it's a long drive—Molly,

leave him alone." When the dog dropped down on all fours, Mitch shook his head at Hunter. "What'd you do, bathe in Eau de Ribeye before you came?"

"He seems to have that effect on women," I said.

"All women?" Hunter asked me, wiping his face off with his shirt. I tried to resist the temptation to look at his chiseled abs, but I failed. And I couldn't even be upset about that, because *wow.*

Jerking my face away before he could catch me looking, I shrugged and said, "The desperate ones," before following Mitch into the building, leaving Hunter to trail behind me.

If I'd thought the outside was gorgeous, the inside was mind-blowing. It was one big open floor plan, an array of furniture and art everywhere you looked. In one corner were elaborate coffee tables. In another there were sculptures. Another section contained chairs of every make and model you could imagine. Huge handcrafted lighting fixtures hung from the ceiling.

"You did all this?" I asked, my eyes wide and taking in every inch.

"Guilty," Mitch said.

"It's incredible. More than worth the drive."

"I appreciate that." A phone rang from somewhere across the room. "Hunter, show her around. I'll be back to check on you in a bit."

"Wow," I said when Mitch walked off. "How have I never heard about this place?"

"Feel free to say it again. 'Hunter, I am so lucky I have you to show me the way.'"

"Oh my gosh, look at these barstools," I said, making my way over to the corner with the seating displays. The seats were shaped like martini glasses, the straw and olive making up the seat back, and each chair was a different color. They were so unique, so funky...*so me.* Hunter had been right. There was no way I could get stuff like this anywhere else, and they were perfect for the new space. "These. I need these."

"Would you rather they be martini-shaped like this, or would you like something closer to your theme? Maybe ice cream cones?"

I think my eyes bugged out of my head. "What? Are you serious? He could make ice cream cone barstools? Please don't tease me."

Hunter laughed. "I'm not teasing. I've never seen him do one, of course, but...I bet if you asked him nicely, he could find a way to do it."

"Oh my God. I think I'm in love."

"It's a little too soon for me, but give me time."

When he winked and walked over to the next section, I let out a groan. "You're completely full of yourself, you know that? Biggest ladies' man I ever met."

Hunter stopped abruptly and turned around, his hands resting on the tables on both sides of me. "You assume a lot."

Swallowing, I said, "Are you trying to tell me I'm

wrong?"

His dark eyes were piercing, his face so close I could feel his breath on my lips. We didn't move, just stood there, eyes locked as I waited for what he would say. My eyes flicked down to his mouth. *Or do.* And suddenly, I wanted nothing more than to press my lips against his, to wrap my arms around his neck and feel him against me.

My breath hitched as he moved infinitesimally closer. There was no indecision, no warring of my brain, just the begging of *do it.* But just as the thought crossed my mind, he backed away, his eyes still on mine as Mitch's voice rang out.

"Sorry about that," the man said. "See anything you like?"

Yeah. Yeah, I do. Looking away from Hunter, I gave Mitch a smile. "I'm a bit overwhelmed. You've got so much great stuff."

"Thank you. We can start narrowing it down if you'll tell me what you need."

I took a deep breath and said, "Do you have some paper? You might wanna write this down."

Four hours later I had designs for my bar, all tables and chairs, lighting, accessories, and—the best part—the ice cream stools. I was squealing inside like a fangirl at a boy band concert over that. Not to mention Mitch had fed us delicious fish tacos, complete with freshly squeezed lemonade. I was in heaven. There was just one teensy tiny little thing left to cover.

"All right," I said, setting down my empty glass. "This is all amazing, and I want it all and more, but let's talk numbers."

Mitch nodded and took a small notepad and pencil out of the front pocket of his shirt. He scribbled down a figure, and when he flashed it my way, my eyes practically fell out of their sockets. There was no way I could afford that. Mitch chuckled and then wrote on the pad again. This time when he showed me, there was a substantial discount, cutting the fee by more than half.

I must've looked confused, because he said, "There's only two people who get that discount, and the other one's my mom."

"You charge your mom?" I said incredulously.

"Nah, she usually ends up paying in meals anyway." He closed the pad and tucked it back into his shirt. "So whaddya say?"

I was pretty sure that question was redundant, because there was no person in their right mind that would've turned an offer like that down. Pulling out my wallet, I said, "I'd say can you start yesterday?"

BY THE TIME we left Mitch's store, it was early evening. I was able to go ahead and take a couple of tall planters, and I was thankful then that I'd relented and let Hunter drive his truck, because there was no way those items would've fit in my Mini's trunk.

I had my seat reclined, my eyes closed, and my hand was out the window, letting the wind roll across my fingertips. With the weight of finding interior pieces for the bar off my shoulders, I felt more relaxed than I had in a while. And they were *great* fucking finds.

"You look happy," Hunter said, and I could hear the smile in his voice.

"I'm ecstatic. Thank you, thank you, thank you. It's beyond what I dared to hope for."

"Good."

"Mitch is a talented guy. How'd you meet him, anyhow?" I asked. When Hunter didn't respond right away, I opened my eyes and saw him rubbing his jaw.

"A mutual friend," he said.

"A mutual friend? That's pretty vague." When he didn't have a response to that, I pushed for more. "Okay, let me guess. You met him through a Craigslist ad and ended up roommates, but he fell in love with the girl you followed here. Then after she caught sight of his glorious hair, it was no contest and you conceded defeat."

He snorted and shook his head.

"What? Am I close?" I asked.

"I'd say you've got a pretty great imagination."

"That's a non-answer."

"Yes, it was."

I got the feeling I shouldn't push for information,

though I wanted to. "You don't like to talk about yourself, do you?"

"A keen observation."

"How are you supposed to let people in if you don't tell them anything?"

He raised an eyebrow at me. "Are you wanting to be let in?"

My face felt sunburned from the heat rushing to it. "I wasn't… I mean, I didn't mean me."

"Maybe I do hold some things close to the vest, but you don't have to know everything about a person's past to really know them."

"But past experiences make up who you are."

"So you're telling me if I asked about your former relationships and all the bad shit you might've gone through when you were younger, that would tell me about the person you are now?" he asked.

"I think it could help explain why some people are the way they are. Take you, for instance. Everything about you screams gorgeous player with a cocky attitude who, other than heartbreaker girl, probably leaves a trail of broken hearts of his own all across the 5 freeway. But then I see the way you run your business, and this responsible, take-no-shit side. And then when you avoid my questions, like now, it shows me another. Something almost vulnerable. You told me I assume things about you, but I think you're more than what you show. I wonder what happened in your life to make you the way you are."

He was silent for a moment, his eyes focused on the road, my words rolling over him. I expected him to say something profound, to open up a little after my speech. Instead, he glanced at me and said, "Gorgeous, huh?"

Cocky. Ass.

"Oh, shut up."

"I CAN GET it," I said, reaching for one of the planters in the bed of the truck. But Hunter lifted it with ease before my hands wrapped around it.

"I don't think so," he said. "Maybe you could unlock your door, though, if you want to keep these upstairs until construction is done."

The thought of Hunter entering my apartment had my stomach doing flips, but what choice did I have? The planters *were* super heavy, and I'd probably drop it or fall down the stairs if I made an attempt.

I tried to remember how I'd left it looking this morning. Were there bras and panties lying around? Did I wash the bowl of oatmeal before I'd left, or would it be sitting on the counter all dried and crusted just waiting for me? His place had been immaculate both times I'd been over there. Oh, what the hell did I care what he thought anyway?

I unlocked the door that led straight up to my place instead of going through the store, and then held it open for him to pass through. After unlocking the door at the top of the stairs and punching in the alarm code—yes, I was anal about safety—I pointed at an open spot he could set it down. Then he headed back to the truck to grab the second one, and I did a quick sweep of the apartment.

Bowl had been washed, no visible undergarments, even made my bed. Looking in the mirror, I pushed back a few windswept strands. I could use some pink gloss, but otherwise, not too shabby after shopping.

"Same spot for this one?" Hunter asked, as his built frame filled the doorway.

"Yeah, thanks."

His body brushed against mine as he moved to the spot I'd indicated, and I couldn't help but check out his ass as he bent over.

Damn. I didn't need to be looking at him, to be memorizing every inch to use later. But I couldn't remember being so sexually attracted to anyone before in my life. Even Cameron, with his dizzying perfection, didn't have me wanting to rip his clothes off and mount him right there on the floor.

"Ryleigh?" I vaguely heard him calling before shaking myself out of my trance. Hunter's forehead was wrinkled in concern. "You okay?"

"Huh? Oh. Yeah. Yeah, I'm okay." I gave a weak smile as I watched him push his hair off his forehead. It was only slightly sweaty—amazing, considering it was about a thousand degrees outside.

"Can I get you something to drink before you go?" I asked.

He seemed surprised by the question. "A water would be great."

"Right. Okay." My damn legs were unsteady as I walked into the kitchen and pulled a couple of water bottles from the refrigerator.

As I shut it, I turned to find him right behind me. He was close, so close. I hadn't bothered to flip on the lights, and it felt...intimate standing there with him like that. But I couldn't find it in myself to move. In fact, I wanted him closer...

He took a step toward me so that the fabric of his shirt grazed my fingers. Then he reached between us, and I swear my heart stopped. Taking one of the waters from my hands, he unscrewed the top and took a long drink, his eyes staying on mine the entire time.

I couldn't move. I couldn't breathe. I knew what my body wanted, but I didn't dare act on it.

But then Hunter took a step closer, and my ass hit the counter. He set down the water and left his hand there, boxing me in between him and the fridge.

"Is there something you want, Ryleigh?" His voice

was barely above a whisper, his eyes searching mine as if he was looking for permission. *Permission for what?*

I opened my mouth to speak, but the words wouldn't come out. I wasn't even sure what I would say if I could. *Please? No? Stop? Kiss me?* None of those felt right, and still I stood there, waiting.

His free hand came up to cup the side of my neck, and his thumb stroked my lower lip. I leaned into his palm, my eyes closing as I relished his touch. Nothing else ran through my mind other than how it felt to be held by him, how warm and strong and virile he was. My lips parted under his fingers…

"Open your eyes."

When I opened them, his head bent down, his lips skimming mine so lightly I would've thought it had been a dream if I wasn't watching it happen. He paused then, not moving away, but waiting…he wanted me to meet him halfway.

With the throbbing between my thighs, and the way every part of me wanted every part of him, there was no way I could refuse, nothing in my brain telling me it was a bad idea, that I should abort mission.

Instead, I closed the gap between us and pressed my lips against his.

And with that, the hesitation between us disappeared.

Hunter's mouth was hungry on mine, more delicious than the sweetest, most sinful fruit from a tree. He kissed me with urgency, like he'd never get the chance to again and this was the moment he'd take with him his whole life. I could feel his soul in that kiss, his passion, and his desire. Desire for *me*.

His hand went to my hair, taking out the clip that held it together before spearing his fingers through the loose strands. I moaned into his mouth, my hands gripping his sides under his shirt and pulling him closer. The way his tongue moved against mine was so wickedly erotic that I knew, if I let him, his tongue between my legs would be something I'd never forget.

He lifted me onto the counter, spreading my legs and positioning himself between them. As he kissed me, his hands rose from my ankles up over my knees. I'd worn a dress today, a flowing one that slid up easy, just as it was doing now…

Hands, warm and rough, grasped the outside of my thighs, and he tore his lips away from mine to rasp, "Tell me this is what you want."

His thumb was massaging slow circles on my skin, his hands inching under my skirt. If I truly didn't want things to go further, this was the time to say it. But there was no way I could stop now. No way in hell I wanted to.

I leaned forward to capture his mouth again, but he pulled away.

"Tell me," he said.

"I want this," I heard myself say, threading my fingers through his hair. "I want you." Pulling his lips back to mine, I kissed him in a way that proved I meant every word. I wrapped my legs around his waist and drew him closer, and his hands went under my dress to my ass, squeezing me tight against him.

His body was rock hard against my needy core, and I ached for friction, from his fingers, his mouth, *his cock…*

As if he'd read my mind, he lifted me off the counter, legs still wrapped around him, and carried me to the first piece of furniture we came to—my oversized lounge chair. He set me down gently, and with one last kiss, he dropped down to his knees, sliding my legs up onto his shoulders. His eyes were fervent, filled with lust, and he licked his lips as he pushed my skirt up around my hips and slipped my panties off.

Oh God. It wasn't nerves I felt then, but the most intense yearning I'd ever felt in my life. If he didn't put his mouth on me then, I'd probably die. I watched him lower his head and lick a path between my thighs. Even with just that brief teasing touch the pleasure was indescribable, and my whole body shivered. The seconds that passed until his lips were on me again were agony, but then his tongue rubbed over my swollen clit, sucking it gently into his mouth.

"Oh my God," I breathed, needing more. My hand came up to grasp his head while the other white-knuckled the arm of the chair. He didn't need any more urging before devouring me, his tongue dipping inside, and then out to flick my clit before diving in again.

His eyes were twinkling with devilry as he watched

me fall apart underneath his mouth. I'd never thought it was hot before to have a guy look at you while they went down on you, but there was nowhere else I wanted his eyes to be. It made the connection flame hotter, more passionate, made me want so much more than his tongue on me and in me.

My body tensed as the rush of an impending orgasm reached its full crescendo before bursting in wave after wave of release. His mouth rode me through it, hungrily sucking every last drop from me. His fingers massaged my legs resting on his shoulders before I dropped them down to the ground. Though my body was thoroughly sated, I craved the feel of him against me.

Sliding off the chair, I sat in his lap with my legs on either side of him and wrapped my arms around his neck. "More," I whispered, before tilting my head to the side and tasting myself on his lips. His arms enveloped me, crushing me to him as his tongue tangled with mine.

Hunter and his magic fucking tongue. If you could capture it and sell it, it'd be worth a fortune.

His cock was hard underneath me, and I circled my hips. A tortured groan escaped him, and then—

The shrill blast of my cell phone ringing and vibrating on the table beside us had me jumping.

"Ignore it," I said, kissing up the side of Hunter's neck.

"Ryleigh."

"It'll stop." I bit his lobe.

He pulled away, his eyes on the phone screen.

Cameron.

It was like being doused with a bucket of ice water. *Cameron* was calling. Cameron, the guy I was supposedly interested in and who was roommates and best friends with the guy I was currently straddling. Without panties.

Oh fuck. *Oh fuck fuck fuck.*

I scrambled off his lap and stared at the phone. Hunter didn't move.

"You should answer it," he said finally.

But I couldn't. How could I answer a call from him after what we'd just…what he'd just…

What did I just do?

The ringing stopped. We looked at each other in silence, but I couldn't read his face. He'd wanted me to answer it? Or was he just saying that to see what I'd do?

With the sexual tension in the room having evaporated the second my phone went off, cold reality slapped us in the face.

What did this mean? Would we be a thing now? Was it just an "oops"? Would he tell Cameron? Would he quit working on renovations and leave me in a lurch?

I couldn't stop the panic from setting in, even though I didn't regret what had just happened.

Wait…I didn't regret it?

I searched for the pangs I knew would be coming, but I felt nothing. In fact, it had all felt so right. The only guilt stemmed from the person on the other end of that line, and that was what had me more confused than anything.

My cell went off again with Cameron's number prominently displayed. When I looked back at Hunter, he seemed resigned, and he stood up.

"I should probably go," he said quietly.

"You don't have to," I told him, getting to my feet.

He ran his hand over his face and then through his hair. "Yeah, I do." He pulled his keys out of his pocket and hesitated before shaking whatever thought he'd had out of his head. Nodding at the phone, he said, "You should probably answer that. I'll see you tomorrow."

And then he left, leaving me standing there in my empty apartment with nothing but a ringing phone and the taste of him on my lips.

Chapter Thirteen
I Left My Hip at Runyon

AFTER A SLEEPLESS night with no idea how to deal with the events of yesterday, I'd called Quinn to talk me off a ledge. Or up the winding incline of Runyon Canyon at six a.m., as it were.

"Oh my God, Ry," Quinn said when I'd finished filling her in on the details. She stopped abruptly, and when I looked over my shoulder, she was gaping at me.

With a sigh, I headed back down the dirt path, the dust kicking up behind me.

"Don't look at me like that. You're supposed to be the nonjudgmental, non-condoning one. That's why I called you."

Quinn pulled her long black ponytail tighter and let her hands drop to her hips. "I'm not judging or condoning, it's just…well, this is *you*."

"I know. I'm a horrible person."

"You are *not* a horrible person," she said, linking her arm through mine as we trudged up the godforsaken hill again. Have I mentioned I hate working out? I especially hate hiking. This should tell you how desperate I was feeling.

"What do I do? Pretend like nothing happened?" I asked.

"First of all, it's not like you're cheating on this Cameron guy. You've been on, what, one date?"

"Technically, but two if you count the reunion."

"And you've never slept with the guy."

"I've never even *kissed* him."

"What?" Quinn stopped again. "Why are we even discussing this whole guilt thing right now?

"Because I *like* Cameron. I've always liked Cameron. I've wanted him since I was fifteen."

She began to drag me up the hill again, which probably looked ridiculous given how damn tiny she was. "Well, you may *like* him, but your body is saying you like *like* this other guy."

"I'm sure my body would like *like* Cameron too if given a chance."

"Just because you've crushed on him since before you knew what sex was doesn't mean you have to still harbor those feelings."

"Oh, but Quinn, he's perfect. So, so perfect. Six four,

the most gorgeous clear blue eyes you've ever seen, a body that could throw you up against the wall—"

"What good's all that if he doesn't use it?"

"—he's polite, he opens doors, he has a job he's passionate about—"

Quinn gave an exaggerated yawn.

"—and he's blond. Hello, I love blond guys."

"Okay, so this guy is *so* perfect. Tell me about Hunter."

"He's…" My mind couldn't stop thinking about the salacious look in his eyes as he knelt between my thighs and the way his hands roamed my body. "Hunter is… He's good with his hands," I finally said.

A snort escaped her. "I bet he is. What else?"

"He's the complete opposite of Cameron. Dark hair, dark eyes, tan, not quite as tall, but super ripped from his job. *That* is what I meant by good with his hands, by the way. Just that he can maneuver a piece of wood."

"Ooh la la, I bet he can."

"I wouldn't know *that*. It didn't go that far. Just—"

"A little pussy nibble, got it."

"Exactly. Hmm," I said. "Pussy nibble…that's a good name for a future shake."

"Make sure it's pink," she said with a wink.

"With lots of cherries."

A smirk crossed Quinn's lips. "I'm guessing from the smile on your face it was pretty damn good."

"It was amazing," I said, groaning. "The man's

tongue is a gift from the gods."

"High fucking five on that." She slapped my raised hand.

We rounded another bend, and when I saw how much farther we had left to go I stopped and clutched my side. "I think I left my hip back there. We should turn around."

"It's worth it at the top. Come on, this is the easy side."

"It's never worth it, and easy my ass."

"Easy ass. You said it, not me. Maybe that should be your mantra," she said, oblivious to the group of guys passing us downhill that were blatantly checking her out.

"I could put it on an apron."

"'Get Licked' seems like enough of an invitation to me."

I wiped the sweat off my brow and looked to my left to see a grey-haired woman with several decades on me speed-walking. She smiled as she passed, and I shot a death glare at Quinn's back. "Remind me to push you off once we reach the top. You healthy people are on crack."

"I'd never be able to eat at your shop if I didn't do this. You're an enabler. I don't know how you're not eight hundred pounds."

"It's called walking around in four-inch heels all day every day."

"No, that's called suicidal."

"Blah blah blah. You're supposed to be helping me."

I moved aside as some crazy yapping dogs off the leash ran past. "Okay, there's something else I need to mention."

Quinn raised an eyebrow. "Why do I get the feeling you're about to drop a bomb?"

"After Hunter left, I answered Cameron's call. He'll be home on Friday."

"And?"

"And he wants to go out that night. Like on a double date."

"No. No, please don't tell me he means with—"

"Hunter. Yeah."

Quinn's eyes grew to the size of saucers. "Pardon my French, but why the *fuck*?"

"They're best friends, and he's been gone for a while. He said it was important for Hunter to get out of the house, go on a date, something something something."

"From the way you've described him, it doesn't sound like the guy needs help in that department."

"My thoughts exactly."

"But you're going? Come on, move your ass. We're almost there." She reached for my arm and didn't let go this time.

"Ugh." At this point, I was ready to crawl the rest of the way. I brushed away the sweaty strands of hair that had somehow come loose and forced my feet to keep going. "Well, I couldn't say no."

"Yes, you could've. You want to see Cameron."

"Yeah."

"*And* Hunter."

"Yes. No. I don't know. Tell me what to do."

When we made it to the top, Quinn faced me and grabbed my shoulders, giving me her best serious face. "Dump Cameron and let him find a cute Barbie to play with. Fuck Hunter until his job is over."

"Quiiiiiiiin," I said, pushing her away as she laughed.

"Hey, that's me telling you what to do. But you don't want that. You just want a sounding board. So in that case I say play it cool until Friday and see how date night goes. Then you'll have a pretty clear answer."

"It's gonna be a clusterfuck, isn't it?" I asked.

"Probably so," she said, climbing up to stand on top of the lone bench overlooking Los Angeles before grabbing my hand to pull me up. "And no offense, but I can't wait to hear all the details."

WHEN HOURS PASSED and there was no sign of Hunter, I did what any woman would do—I tracked him down.

No, not in a creepy stalker way, I mean he *was* only next door. But the silence was deafening, and I had to make sure we were…good.

He was outside the store, clipboard in hand, and checking things off as his team carried supplies inside. When he glanced up at where I hesitated on the sidewalk, a small smile curved his lips, though I couldn't see his eyes through his sunglasses.

"Mornin'," he said.

"No 'sunshine' to go along with that?" I teased.

"Nah, I'd call you something different today."

"Oh yeah? And what would that be?"

His grin grew wider, but he shook his head, looking back down at the pad in his hands and making a notation. "Hey, T," he called out. "Can you make sure Noel has the updated blueprint tacked to the wall?"

"On it," a man with a buzzcut said, slapping him on the back.

"Thanks." Hunter looked back at me and pushed his sunglasses on top of his head. And just like that, I remembered why I'd kissed him yesterday and why I'd let him kiss me back—in several hidden places. He was just so fucking gorgeous. His eyes seemed darker today, though no less potent, and I longed to run my fingers through his hair again.

"Was there something you needed from me?" he asked.

Yes. Yes, there was. But it was nothing I should be asking for.

"I just…hadn't seen you today and I…um," I stammered. *God, just spit it out.* "Well, I just wanted to make sure everything is…good. With you."

He squinted in the bright sun and his hand came up

to shield his face as he studied me for what felt like minutes. Then he dropped his hand and said, "Yeah. Yeah, I'm good. We're good."

Relief swept through me. "Great. Um. Happy to hear it."

"And you?"

"Fine here too."

"You sure?" His brow furrowed. "You looked like you were hobbling a bit."

"Hobbling? Oh. I went hiking this morning. Remind me never to do that again."

"Not a fan of the great outdoors?"

"Not a fan of exercise in general, no."

"Noted," he said.

I kicked at a pebble with the toe of my wedge and tried to find something else to say. I knew what I *wanted* to talk about, but I wasn't sure how the hell I was supposed to bring that up. Being at a loss for words wasn't something I was used to, and I had a feeling it was the same for him.

Yeah, this was not awkward at all.

"So," I said.

"So."

I wanted to know if he'd agreed to Friday, but I didn't have to ask. I could see it in his eyes. And the look I found there made me want to call the whole thing off.

"Hunter—"

He cleared his throat and looked down at his clipboard. "The first round of furniture orders will be here in two weeks, and I'll make sure we're in good enough shape to start moving things in. We'll just need to touch base on the timeline once Mitch gives me firm dates on when you can expect the rest of your shipment."

"I just want to say—"

"I've got to run out for an appointment in just a few minutes, so if you need anything, let T know," he said, nodding to the man he'd spoken to earlier.

"Oh. Everything okay?" I asked.

"Yep." He stuck the pen over his ear and looked past me. "Well, I should probably get back to it."

"Right. Yeah, okay." I moved aside so he could make his way into the store. As he passed, I wanted to reach out and grab his shirt, pull him back to me. But of course I didn't do that.

"Wait—Hunter?"

He stopped and then turned around. I found myself opening and closing my mouth several times, nothing wanting to come out. As if he sensed what I was trying to get out, he walked toward me, closing the gap between us.

"No regrets, okay, Ryleigh?" he said. "None."

Chapter Fourteen
I Must Be Stupid

CAMERON DIDN'T REALIZE he was making a massively bad decision when he'd organized a double date with all of us. He wanted his best friend and his…well, whatever I was, to celebrate his work success, and what could we do, say no?

But there was a sick feeling in the pit of my stomach, one I knew would only grow once I was in the same room with Hunter. It had to have been a mistake, what had happened between the two of us, one brought on by some kind of twisted case of lust. Why my body was betraying my mind, I had no idea, but now that Cameron was back, I was determined to put the past few weeks out of my head and start fresh. Even though technically we weren't exclusive, I still felt guilty, no matter what Quinn said. Hell, I couldn't even bring myself to tell Shayne and Paige, so that had to mean something.

I had put my hair half up that night and made sure to bring a cardigan, remembering the last time we went out and the freezing, not-quite-sexy scene at the beach. I'd told myself things would be different tonight. Just a casual, fun time with friends and a guy I'd still like to kiss one of these days. Besides, Hunter was bringing a date too, so it wasn't like it'd be some awkward threesome.

"Remind me not to leave you for so long next time. I missed the view," Cameron said when he opened the passenger door and pulled me to my feet. He laced his fingers through mine and smiled as we made our way into La Trattoria. It was a gorgeous night, one of the many perks of living in Southern California. We chose a table outside on the veranda, strands of yellow lights and ivy hanging from the wooden lattice above us. It was intimate, but jovial, the sound of laughter and the scent of Italian spices permeating the air.

"I'm regretting inviting anyone else," Cameron said as he laid his arm on the back of my chair. "I think I should call them and cancel."

I was about to respond when a familiar head of hair caught my eye. Hunter was heading toward the table, accompanied by a brunette in a very tight, very short red minidress.

You've got *to be kidding me. Is that his type?*

"Too late," Cameron said, following my gaze, before

standing and greeting Hunter with a clap on the back. I stayed right where I was, still looking at the short hem of the girl's dress. If she bent over, the whole restaurant would get a nice view, there was no doubt about that. Under the dimmed lights, her deep tan looked almost orange, or at least that's what I was telling myself. Okay, so she was kind of pretty, even though most people would look skankalicious in something like that.

"Hey, Ryleigh," Hunter said, nodding at me without smiling. "Ryleigh, this is Cassidy, Cassidy, Ryleigh." And that was as far as the introductions went before he sat down and waved down a waiter to order a bottle of wine for the two of them. Red wine.

"I'll have a double Grey Goose, straight, and a..." Cameron looked at me expectantly.

"Oh, I'll have a, um..." I scanned over the drink menu, trying to find something that wasn't wine or pure vodka.

"She'll have a frozen peach bellini," Hunter said, his eyes focused on the food menu in front of him.

I smiled at the waiter. "A frozen peach bellini would be great. Thank you."

"Looks like I've got to catch up on your tastes," Cameron said. "I've never had one of those. Mind if I try yours?"

"Absolutely you can have a taste," I said.

Hunter coughed and reached for his water, taking a long swallow before stretching out his arm over the back of his date's chair. "So how was Hong Kong? Congrats on the funding. I had a feeling you'd put up a hard fight."

Laughing, Cameron said, "You know I don't like to be told no. Had to wear the fuckers down, but it happened."

"What is it you do?" Cassidy asked, causing Cameron to launch into a long spiel about what his work entailed. I was half listening, my eyes drifting over to Hunter, who had picked up the menu again. He looked up then and caught me staring, and his eyes flickered with some emotion I couldn't put my finger on. Whatever that look was, I had a feeling it didn't mean anything good. Would he tell Cameron what happened? No, I didn't think so. Would he end up at Cassidy's house later? Now *that* was the more probable possibility. And it made me sick to think about.

"…and Ryleigh owns an ice cream shop."

"Oh how cute," Cassidy said. "Do you have anything vegan there?"

I tried not to wrinkle my nose. Healthy ice cream was my worst nightmare. It was so wrong on every level. And don't get me started on the damn vegans. "Uh, no. The more chocolate and cream I can throw in the mixer, the better."

"That's a shame. I bet it'd sell really well."

I bet it wouldn't. Instead of getting into a debate with the non-sugar-eating size zero across from me, I plastered a tight smile on my face, and said, "Maybe."

The waiter came around with the drinks then. Perfect timing.

"Speaking of Licked, how's it looking?" Cameron asked. "Grand opening's coming soon, right?"

"Oh God, don't remind me." I took a long sip of the bellini and tried not to think about how crazy the next few weeks would be, or that I'd be the owner of not one store, but two. With the potential to spin off a few chains, if the show went well and I received the majority of viewer votes. Nope, not thinking about that at all. *Hmm, this drink is amazing…*

"That bad? Hunter, I thought you had things worked out over there?" Cameron said.

"I do—"

"He does—"

Hunter and I looked at each other when we both answered at the same time.

"Sorry, I didn't mean *that* part was oh God," I said. "Hunter and his team have killed it. There wouldn't be a store without him. And definitely not one ready a few short weeks from now." My cheeks warmed, whether from sucking down half of my drink so fast or from admitting that I needed Hunter in some part of my life. I wondered if they could all see right through me.

"Thank you," Hunter said quietly. He swirled the wine in his glass before raising it. "A toast, shall we? To Cameron and Ryleigh's successful ventures, my impeccable *taste*, and Cassidy's"—he winked at the woman next to him—"short little skirt."

Cameron laughed and clinked his glass with

Hunter's. "Cheers to that."

Swallowing thickly, I raised my glass and cheered along with them even as the bile went up my throat.

Stupid, I know. What did I care if Hunter went out with that woman? Or *any* woman. I had a stunningly handsome man to my left, and this moment was one I'd dreamed about a thousand times. Although in my dream I didn't have a knot in my stomach. And I wasn't trying to avoid giving anyone at the table an evil eye.

The waiter came around to take our orders, and I glanced at the menu, even though there was no need. I always got the same thing at Italian places.

"And for you, miss?" the waiter asked, his accent super thick and pronounced, though it sounded slightly off to my ears. *An actor practicing, I bet.* "I'll have the cheese ravioli, please."

"No way," Cameron said. "You have to get something better than that. The conchiglie with clams and mussels is amazing. Or maybe the saltimbocca alla Romana."

"Um." The guy had been eating crazy food in Hong Kong too long. We didn't know each other well enough for him to get that I didn't like to venture outside my comfort foods, but that wasn't his fault. I could feel Hunter's eyes on me, waiting for my response. "No, I think the ravioli is more my style," I said, handing the menu to the waiter before smiling at Cameron. "But thank you for the suggestions."

"You're missing out," he told me. "But you can try

mine."

Hunter's lips twisted as he closed his menu and finished off his glass of red.

"Hey, if you guys are free on Sunday there's a Walk for Wounded Vets event my company signed up for. I'd love it if you could join us."

Okay, other than vegan ice cream, exercise was up there on my all time please-don't-make-me-do-it list. But then Cameron said wounded vets, and if I said no that would make me a heartless bastard.

"We've actually got to get a few things set up on Sunday, so that might not work out," Hunter chimed in, saving me from making up an excuse. I tried to get his attention to silently thank him, but he wouldn't meet my eyes.

"I'd love to join," Cassidy said. "I'm *all* about philanthropy."

Cameron tilted his head to the side. "Is that right. And how did you meet Hunter again?"

"Well, it's a little embarrassing," she said, before taking a sip of her wine and beaming at Hunter. "I saw him on this list at a matchmaking place, and I just knew we'd hit it off."

I almost dropped my glass. "Matchmaking place…you wouldn't mean HLS, would you?"

"That's the one," she said, giving me a broad smile. "How'd you know?"

There was no way Shayne had given her Hunter's

info, so I played a hunch. "Well, who doesn't know Val?"

"I know, right? She is *so* glamorous for her age. When I'm that old, I hope I look that good."

It took biting my lip hard enough to draw blood to keep from laughing. If Val heard her say that, the only thing she would've given this girl is a stiletto up her ass.

"Matchmaker," Cameron said, a wrinkle forming between his brows as he studied his friend. "You signed up with a matchmaking service? And Ryleigh mentioned you went to an event or something."

Hunter drank half of his second glass of wine before responding. "It's a long story," he said before looking directly at me. "Ryleigh's fault."

What? Like I'd been the one to push him at Val and force him to join the mixer. Or accept a date with the miniature Val across from me.

Cameron looked at me expectantly for an explanation.

"Uh…" I had no idea what to say to that. "I'm not sure how I'm responsible for this coupling, but you're welcome, I guess."

"Aw, take some credit," Hunter said, throwing his arm around the back of Cassidy's chair. "Do we look as good together as the two of you do?"

What the hell was wrong with him? *Shut up,* my eyes screamed, but it was like Cameron had read my mind.

"What's going on with you?" he asked.

"Not sure what you mean. I'm just relaxing with my

best friend and his girl, and this pretty little thing. We may not have much in common, but hey, what does that matter?" He finished off his second glass and reached for the bottle, but Cameron grabbed it first.

"I think you need to lay off wine and apologize to her."

Hunter looked dead at me. "I apologize, Ryleigh."

"Not to her," Cameron said. "To your *date*."

"Oh, he doesn't need to say he's sorry for calling me pretty," Cassidy said, nuzzling in closer to Hunter. "You can do it again if you want."

You could cut the sudden tension in the room with a knife as Cameron stared at Hunter, who didn't back down from his gaze. There seemed to be a whole conversation taking place between the two of them that we weren't privy to.

After the entrees were passed around we ate in uncomfortable silence. I didn't know what to say, or if anything I uttered would be welcome. Cassidy, on the other hand, had no problem babbling on about herself and didn't mind that no one was responding to anything she said. She was a one-woman show.

I considered both men in between bites of my ravioli. On one hand, there was Cameron, with his apparent nice-guy persona and stunning good looks. I hadn't even gotten a real chance to get to know him yet, but from what I'd seen so far...we got along great, but were we even compatible as anything more than friends? Was there sexual chemistry?

Every chance at a kiss and anything after had blown up in our faces, and it almost felt like a sign.

Then there was Hunter. Darker in looks and personality, but with an unbeatable sense of humor and a possessive quality to him that was sexy—and dangerous—as hell. He seemed to just *get* me in a way not even some of my closest friends did. But he also scared me to death—was he just a playboy out for a good time?

As I looked between them both, I knew that any woman would be lucky to have a chance with either of them. *How the hell did* I *get in this position?* And would there even *be* a decision to make after tonight? I knew firsthand how important friendships were, especially in my own life, so how could I use such bad fucking judgment? There was no way I would let myself be a Yoko Ono in any situation.

But one thought still nagged at me: If I were truly honest with myself, which guy would I choose? The man I'd always wanted? Or the man I'd never forget?

I pondered that for the rest of the dinner. When the check came, the two guys battled over it for two minutes before I quietly slipped the waiter my credit card and let them continue to carry on over who would pay. Alpha dogs at their finest. They didn't take too kindly to the fact that I had paid the bill—I know, such gentleman, right?—but I was so ready to get out of there.

"I'm so sorry about that," Cameron said as he opened the passenger door for me. Before I slid inside, I caught Hunter's eyes from across the parking lot. The look I saw there sent a pang straight through my heart. *Don't go home with him*, they said. *Don't choose him.*

Fuck. I could never unsee that look.

"It's a nice night. Want to try the beach again?" Cameron asked when he got in the car. "I promise there's no chance of rain tonight. I looked."

My gaze was still on Hunter's truck as it pulled out of the parking lot. *Where is he going? He wouldn't go to Cassidy's place…would he?*

"Ryleigh?" Cameron asked again.

I gave him a thin smile. "A walk on the beach sounds great."

HE'D BEEN RIGHT; it was a gorgeous night. Not too cold, no smell of rain in the air. It was the perfect date.

Then why does it feel so wrong?

He took my hand in his and we walked down to the water, the sand feathery soft under my feet.

"I'm sorry again for whatever that was at dinner," Cameron said. "I've never seen Hunter act like that."

Never? "It's fine. Really. Maybe he just had a bad day. Or maybe Cassidy was grating on his nerves already."

"It could be that. She's not his type at all."

My ears perked up. Not his type? What was his type? I wanted to ask, but thankfully common sense kicked in and

I kept my mouth shut.

"So…no more trips for a while?" I asked.

"Nah. The film is based here, so now that we've got enough funding, we can get started on the fun stuff."

"The not begging for money stuff, you mean."

A laugh rumbled from his chest. "That's exactly what I mean."

The farther we strolled down the beach, the more it felt as though the heavy weight of tension was fading, being swept away with the rolling tide. Cameron's thumb rubbed back and forth over mine, and I waited for the words he was working himself up to say.

"I'm not sure if I told you before, but you look beautiful tonight."

"Thank you," I said, laying my head on his arm. "You always say the nicest things." And he really did. In fact, I couldn't find any faults with him at all, other than the weird feeling in the pit of my stomach whenever we were alone. But that had to be nerves and the anticipation of the first kiss that I knew had to be coming sometime this century.

And then he pulled me around in front of him, and I saw that look again. The it's-really-gonna-happen-this-time-so-you-better-buckle-up-and-kiss-me-long-and-hard look.

Finally. It was really happening this time. No rain, no blaring alarms, no freezing wind…nothing in the world to interrupt us.

His hand left mine as he cradled my face. "I've been

wanting to do this for a long time."

"Me too," I said honestly.

As he leaned down, I stood up on my tiptoes to meet him. *Please feel something. Please let this be right.* His lips met mine softly, once, twice. Then my mouth parted for his tongue, my head tilting to the side as we tasted each other.

And it was wrong.

So wrong.

It wasn't even his kiss, which under normal circumstances would be fucking amazing. My body screamed out, red warning flags flashing all around us that this wasn't right. *Why? Why, why, why can I not have this?*

When you've wanted someone for so long, it only made sense that it was for a good reason. It wasn't supposed to be a big stop sign and Frankie Goes to Hollywood's "Relax" blaring through your mind. It was supposed to be passion and fireworks and the all-encompassing feeling of rightness. Instead, I felt…lips. And tongue. The physical act of kissing that had no impact on me whatsoever.

"Cameron…" I said as I pulled away.

He sighed and dropped his hands. "I know."

"I can't do this. I'm sorry, I just…can't."

He stared at me, his sky blue eyes searching mine. Then he looked away, and with another deep sigh he nodded. "I had a feeling this was coming."

He did? It wasn't just me? Or maybe it was me, and I was losing my mind.

"You did?"

"I'm not a completely oblivious guy."

"No, you're amazing," I said. "Perfect, really, but I just…" How the hell was I supposed to say, *You're just not three inches shorter with brown fuck-me eyes and a magic tongue*?

"You don't have to explain."

"I know I don't, but I want to."

Cameron gave a small chuckle. "Look, Ryleigh, you're incredible. Beautiful. Smart. The whole package. You don't have anything to explain or apologize for."

I groaned. "See, then you go and say something utterly perfect that makes me want to rip all your clothes off."

He raised an eyebrow. "Really?"

"Okay, maybe more of like…a high five."

With a laugh, he ran his hands up and down my arms. "You should find someone you want to do more than high-five with. In fact, I think maybe you already have."

I froze. *Did he know? There's no way he could know.*

"I'm playing a hunch here," he continued, "but I saw the way Hunter looked at you tonight when he thought I wasn't paying attention. And the way you kept glancing at him too."

"But that doesn't—"

"Not to mention he was not himself at all. And he knew what you'd want to drink. He knew without even knowing you what you'd want your bar to look like." He stopped and rubbed his jaw before shaking his head. "I can't compete with that."

"You don't have to—"

"I know." Cameron gave me a sad smile. "But I love that guy like my own brother, and I've seen the shit he's gone through. If you're the one he wants, I'd never stand in the way of that. Especially if I know it's reciprocated."

My heart was about to explode out of my chest. Was he *giving me permission* to date his best friend? Was this some kind of alternate universe? Had I eaten hallucinogens at dinner? But more to the point—how did he see all that when Hunter and I hadn't?

I picked my jaw up off the sand, tears blurring my vision. "I don't even know what to say. I'm so sorry. I'm the worst kind of person—"

"No, you're not."

"I am. I'm repulsive. Like Vegemite."

"Hey, some of us like that stuff." He brushed away a tear rolling down my cheek. Great, now he was comforting me? *I am an asshole. Grade-A major asshole.*

"I need you to stop being so good about this," I said, sniffling. "You're supposed to be devastated. It's killing my fragile ego."

"Your ego? You just told me you want to give me a high five."

A small chuckle escaped my lips as I wiped the rest of the wetness from my face. "Good point."

We both looked down at the ground, unsure of what to say. Though part of me hated to let go of him, the relief I felt, like a weight off my shoulders, had eased. How could you want something so badly yet every part of your body screamed out against it?

"You know…I never told you this," Cameron said quietly, "but I used to watch you."

My head jerked up. "When?"

"At school. Every morning you came in through the east wing door. My homeroom and locker were right outside of it, and I couldn't help but notice you as you passed. You didn't look like anyone else. Which was a good thing, don't think it wasn't. But you were different, and it caught my eye. You lit up the halls when you walked through those doors. So pretty. So confident."

Stunned. That was the only word that came to mind in that moment. "I didn't know you'd ever noticed me," I said in a small voice.

"I did."

I swallowed and met his eyes. There was something akin to regret in them. But why?

"You sat at the same table during lunch period. Always with a drumstick ice cream cone, which makes sense now," he said, with a hint of a smile. "But you seemed like a different girl during lunch than the one I saw walk in every morning. You smiled and talked with your friends, but whatever happened in the hours in between obviously wore on you."

How did he see that? The insecurity I'd felt during that awkward stage in my life, the teasing and taunts, the dirty looks. No matter how much I'd moved on, I could still feel the seventeen-year-old Ryleigh inside me. The one who worried about what others thought of her. The one who secretly wanted so desperately to fit in but couldn't no matter how hard I tried. So I'd stopped trying then. And when graduation came, I'd suddenly felt free.

"School…wasn't easy," I said.

"I'm sorry."

"Not your fault."

"Yeah, it is." When my brow creased, he continued, "I never talked to you. You think I didn't know you existed, but I knew. And what did I do about it? I saw a beautiful girl struggling, and I heard what people said, but what did I do to help her? Nothing."

I opened my mouth to speak, but the words didn't come out. What could I say? That it didn't matter? That he was wrong?

"Coward. I was a coward, Ryleigh."

"No," I said, crossing my arms tight over my chest. "You weren't. That's just how high school is for some people. Not everyone has a great experience."

"But I wonder if… Well, what if—"

Holding up my hand, I said, "No point in what-ifs. Trust me on that one."

"All I'm trying to say is, I wish I'd seen you. Really seen you. Because you deserve that. And if Hunter's the guy who sees all of you…well, he deserves that too."

The sting of tears behind my eyes again had me looking back down at my feet so he wouldn't notice.

Dammit, I wasn't going to be a complete crybaby, but his words eased the vulnerable teenager that still cared what others thought of her.

"Thank you, Cameron," I whispered. "That means a lot." He gave me a sad smile, and dammit, a traitorous tear escaped down my cheek. Wiping it away, I sniffed and said, "Can I high-five you now?"

CAMERON DROVE US back in relative silence except for the radio playing low in the background and the occasional small talk I knew he was making to help me feel better about the situation. I wondered if I'd see him again, or if he'd want to see me. Maybe he'd come in the shop and order the Heartbreak Special that I was currently piecing ingredients together for in his honor.

After he kissed me goodbye on the cheek, I got out of Cameron's car and, feeling dejected, decided to grab some comfort ice cream downstairs before heading to my apartment. I unlocked the door and turned back to wave. He nodded at me, and, after a moment, drove away. Watching his car fade into the distance, I felt two things—the first being disheartened that I'd been so close to getting what I wanted and had sabotaged everything. Cameron was perfect. So damn perfect. Which led to the second thing I was feeling—relief. Because he clearly wasn't what my mind, heart, or body wanted. And wasn't that just a kick in the pants.

With a sigh, I entered the shop, and as I turned to close and lock the door, a hand shot out and held it open. I jumped in shock as, without a word, Hunter slid inside and stood toe to toe with me. His eyes were intense on mine as he took the key out of my hand, turned, and locked the door.

I WAS STILL so shocked to see him that I couldn't process what he'd just done. Then he tossed my key on the counter and began to circle me slowly, his eyes never leaving mine.

"What are you doing here, Hunter?" I asked, forcing the words out. I could barely breathe; just having him there in front of me, his jaw tight, was enough to suck all the air from the room.

He'd unbuttoned the top of his shirt, and it looked like he'd dragged his hand through his hair more than a few times. The effect was so damn hot that my heart beat a faster rhythm in my chest. When he didn't answer, I tried again, my voice coming out in a whisper this time. "Why are you here?"

He stopped circling me then.

"You can't be with him." Unlike mine, his tone was strong, demanding. Unyielding.

Lifting my chin at his words, I said, "What makes you think you have any right to tell me what I can and can't do?"

"I mean it," he said, walking toward me, and I found myself backing away from his approach. "He's not right for you."

That lit a fire within me. It made me crazy that he seemed to know what I wanted before even I knew. Even if he *did* happen to be right, I didn't want to give him the satisfaction. Yet.

"Why? Because you know everything about me? Just like you know what I drink and what kind of furniture I like. Does that make *you* right for me?" I laughed. I couldn't help myself. It was hysterical, undone laughter, but it was also desperate. I didn't want to acknowledge the truth of that statement so easily, not when I wasn't sure what his intentions were. Instead, I lobbed a grenade in his direction. "What happened to Cassidy? I'm sure she was hoping for a nightcap. She was certainly dressed for it."

"I don't give a fuck about what she wants."

"It didn't seem that way to me."

He stopped advancing and narrowed his eyes at me. "We both know that's not true."

Crossing my arms across my chest, I said, "It's not my business what you do. Or don't do."

"Isn't it? You want me to walk out that door and go

back to her place?"

Hell no. "If that's what you want."

"Fuck that."

I shivered, even though I didn't feel cold in the slightest. The opposite, actually. "It's late. You should go."

"Is that what you want?" he asked, moving toward me again until I could feel his body brush up against mine. "You want me to leave?"

But I hesitated, so even when I whispered, "Yes," my body betrayed me.

One of his hands went to my waist as the other cupped my neck. "Why aren't you with Cameron tonight?"

I should've pulled away and put up more of a fight. I didn't want to melt like butter in this man's arms, to let him know I was his for the taking. But the words tumbled out of my mouth anyway. "It's over."

Hunter went still. "Say that again."

"It's over with Cameron. We ended things toni—" I didn't even get the words out before his mouth was on mine, his kiss burning with possession. The passion I'd felt when I'd tasted him before was back, setting my body on fire as he backed me against the wall. His body pressed firmly against mine, his erection growing hard against my stomach as we devoured each other, our tongues tangling in a sensuous dance, and his hand gripping the back of my neck. My hands threaded through his hair, pulling him closer, but even that wasn't close enough. As if he'd read my mind, he hitched one of my legs around his waist, his hand traveling underneath the dress to grab my ass. Then he stepped closer, rubbing his hard length between my thighs.

I moaned into his mouth, and that only encouraged him to grind against me again.

"Oh my God," I said on a breath as his lips found my neck. *Yes.* This…this was how it felt when it was right. Tightening my leg around his waist, I circled my hips and let my head fall back against the wall. I wanted the feel of his fingers inside me, needed the explosion I knew would happen when he touched me.

"Tell me." Hunter's lips brushed mine. "Tell me to touch you."

Rubbing myself against him again, I leaned forward to capture his mouth, but he pulled back. "Please," I said, not even caring in that moment that I was begging for it. "Please put your hands on me—"

Hunter's mouth met mine again, his kiss hungry as he reached down between us with his free hand and pushed aside my panties. His fingers slid between my sensitive lips before one of them slipped inside. I was wet, so wet, and when he added a second finger, I couldn't help the "fuck" that came out of my mouth. His mouth swallowed my curse as the pressure began to build. Spearing my hand through his hair again, I squeezed his fingers, and this time, he groaned and removed his hand.

"Upstairs," he said. "Now."

Thirty seconds later we were in my apartment, the door kicked shut and Hunter's lips on my neck. His hand went to my hair, pulling the clip out so that it tumbled over my shoulders.

"Like this with me," he said. "I want you to let your hair down with me."

"Yes," I breathed into his mouth, as I unbuttoned the rest of his shirt, pulling it off his shoulders. He hadn't worn anything underneath, and the sight of him bare-chested in the middle of my apartment made me want to pinch myself. He was here. With me. Wanting to be with *me.*

With his crumpled shirt in my hands, I backed down the hall, daring him to follow. He answered with a savage grin, stalking forward as I entered my bedroom. I tossed his shirt over my lounge chair by the window as he stood in the doorway unbuckling his belt and the top button of his pants.

"Stop," I said, and he paused. The look he was giving me was making me brave as I went to stand in front of him, pushing his hands away and lowering his zipper myself. There wasn't a hesitant bone in my body, no warning bells. The only flutter I felt was from anticipation of getting this man naked and in my bed.

I slipped my hands under the sides of his boxer briefs, and as I pushed them down his thighs, I went to my knees. His long, thick cock pointed proudly in my direction, hard and ready for me. Looking up at Hunter, I wrapped my fingers around the base and ran my tongue over the tip. He took a shuddering breath, his eyes intently watching. Sucking the head into my mouth, I heard him groan, which only spurred me on to take him deeper.

"Ryleigh…fuck." He grabbed my hair as my tongue ran along the underside of him. Then I pushed my lips down his entire length, taking as much of him as I could. He tasted better than any creamy concoction I could've dreamed up. I know that sounds ridiculous because that's never true, but in Hunter Morgan's case, it was totally fucking true. Like a delicious mixture of toffee and sea salt, the two flavors balancing to make one heady combination, and I couldn't get enough.

"Christ, woman," he said, his hand in my hair tightening. "You have to stop before I come." When I grinned and sucked him again, my hand twisting up and down the wet path my mouth had made all over his rock-hard cock, he growled and pushed my head back. "Get on the bed," he said through clenched teeth.

Loving the effects of the sexual torment I'd put him through, I went over to the bed and put one knee on it. Glancing over my shoulder to see Hunter removing his clothes and shoes, I said, "I might need your help getting out of this dress."

I couldn't take my eyes off the physical wonder that was Hunter fully naked. His eyes gleamed in the dark, watching me take him in as he ripped open a foil packet with his teeth. His broad shoulders and chest led down to abs that could've been carved from stone. The deep V of his hips showcased the most beautiful—yes, beautiful—cock I'd ever seen, and his muscular legs were perfect for, well, thrusting. A shot of lust ran through me at the thought.

"You need some help, you said…" After rolling the condom on, Hunter came to stand behind me and kissed my shoulder before unzipping my dress. It dropped to the ground, and I kicked it off and turned to face him. His lips covered mine as he held my waist, backing us onto the bed so his body pinned me to the mattress.

Kisses rained down my neck, my chest, over my covered breasts, and then Hunter sat up, pushing my legs wide so he could kneel between them. He lifted my ankle to his shoulder, and smoothed his hand down to tease my thighs before moving it back up my calves. "I think we should keep these on," he said, fingering my strappy peacock-blue stilettos. "But everything else is coming the fuck off."

He placed a hot kiss on the inside of my ankle, his lips leisurely making their way up my leg, and I swear goose bumps broke out all over my body. When he reached my inner thigh, his nose grazed my soaked panties, and I jerked as need spiked through me.

"Mind if I take these?" he asked, his lips moving to place featherlight kisses over the useless lace covering me. *Off. Take them the hell off.*

His teeth skimmed along my lower stomach, and I lifted my hips as he bit down on the edge of my panties and began to drag them off me. Using his mouth. Only his mouth.

And *holy shit,* that was the hottest thing I'd ever seen in my life.

When they were discarded on the floor, he crawled back over me, one hand reaching underneath my back to unhook my bra. It was gone in a flash, and his mouth was on my breast, licking my nipple to a stiff peak before taking it inside his mouth. My back arched, I lost my breath, and the feel of him hard and ready against my stomach had me squirming. My hands weaved through his hair as my hips moved to find his, needing the friction to soothe the ache only he could fill.

"So impatient," he said, smiling against my other breast before taking me into his mouth again.

"Please, Hunter." I felt the tip of his cock at my core, and I lifted up, wanting nothing more than for him to slide inside, fill me, and fuck me until morning. "I can't wait this time."

"Mmm...*this time*." His lips moved up to mine, a wicked gleam in his eyes as I lay there panting underneath him. "Since you asked so nicely..."

With his hand on my waist, he lined our hips up and pushed inside me, slow and steady, drawing out the sensation of feeling each other for the first time. A sigh escaped my lips; I wanted to hold him there, to keep him in between my thighs where he belonged.

"So good... *Fuck*." Leaning down over me, he backed his hips up and took my mouth again, his tongue dipping inside at the same time his cock plunged into me.

I rode the waves of pleasure, my nails running down his back. I pulled him closer, needing him deeper. His gaze never left mine, and I realized I needed it—needed that connection with him. The all-consuming physical pleasure combined with what his eyes were conveying without saying a word. This wasn't a casual fuck for him. It meant more than he'd wanted to let on. *I* meant more. And that knowledge had the last of my reserve dissipating, giving myself over to him completely.

The strong legs I'd admired earlier propelled his hips forward, the pressure in my lower body building, and the need to release urgent and imminent. When he pushed inside again, I clenched my muscles around his cock. It took him by surprise because his movements became jerky and he started to ride me harder, more desperate, driving us both toward the brink.

As the pressure built, he reached between us and stroked my clit, and that was all it took. An orgasm ripped through me so strong I could only gasp, unable to even cry out his name. As my body continued to shudder from the intensity of the mind-shattering climax, Hunter fisted his hand in my hair and came, long and hard, inside me. His lips crushed mine, swallowing our moans as our hips rocked gently, neither of us wanting to make the move to leave the other. He could stay there, sleep there, live there if he wanted to.

And damn I wanted him to.

His kisses grew softer, his teeth nipping my lips as our bodies stilled in the tangled sheets.

"Ryleigh?" he asked, still inside me, still pressing

kisses along my jaw.

"Hmm?" I tried to keep my eyes open, but a sense of satiated peace had settled in my bones, making it hard not to fall asleep in his arms.

"I'm keeping you," he said, his voice low and sincere.

A lazy smile crossed my lips.

I felt the loss of him immediately when he pulled out, but he quickly discarded the condom and was back in the bed and drawing me against his side. He pulled me half on top of him, his strong arms wrapping around me and his fingers running through my hair. I kissed his chest and snuggled closer, letting sleep overtake me, completely content in that moment to just be.

I was wrong when I'd said Cameron was perfect. No, this…lying on top of Hunter and listening to his heartbeat…*this* was perfection.

Chapter Sixteen

Buuuusted

WHEN I WOKE up the next morning, it felt as though I'd emerged from the hottest dream of my life. I snuggled into my pillow, calling to mind the handsome face of the man who'd kept me more than satisfied all night. Stretching my legs out, I rubbed one against the long, hairy leg under mine.

Wait. Leg?

My eyes flipped open, and a pair of warm brown ones stared at me from the pillow next to mine.

"Mornin', sunshine," he said.

Not. A. Dream.

"Hi," I said shyly, pulling the covers up to my chin to cover, well, everything.

He chuckled. "No need to do that."

"I thought I dreamed you."

"You didn't, so let's maybe get rid of this," he said, inching the sheet back down my back.

I let him leave it wherever he wanted. *After all, look at the view he's giving me,* I thought, as my eyes trailed down to where the covers lay just under his pelvis. *Damn.*

"Sleep well?' he asked.

"I don't recall sleeping much. I think a certain someone kept me awake most of the night."

He smiled, brushing the hair off my back before running his fingers softly across my skin. *Wow, he is gorgeous to wake up to.* I hoped there wasn't makeup smeared all over my face, but I was pretty sure it had come off at some point during one of our sweaty romps.

"You're fucking stunning first thing in the morning."

"Oh no." I hid my face in the pillow and shook my head.

"What's oh no? I'm not allowed to say that?"

"No, you're not allowed to lie," I said, but I couldn't keep the cheesetastic grin off my face.

"I'd never lie to you." He took my hand and kissed my fingertips, and my heart skipped. Sexy *and* a romantic? It was almost too much to ask for.

"I didn't want to wake you, but I need to get going soon. Take a shower, grab my work clothes. Don't wanna be late and piss off the boss woman."

"I think she'd be lenient on you."

"Not if I miss her deadline by staying in her bed all

day. Though it might be worth it."

"Might?" I said, feigning shock. "*Might* be worth it? You better retract that statement, Mr. Morgan."

He pulled me on top of him, his body warm and his erection stirring.

"Mmm, you're just starting trouble now, mister. I thought you had to leave."

"I do."

"Okay. See you later, then."

"See you."

He didn't budge, just grinned up at me with a look that would've singed my panties had I been wearing any.

"I suppose I could make you coffee before I send you on your way," I said.

"If we *have* to get out of bed, then I guess I'll settle for that."

I gave him a quick peck on the lips. "The good creamer is downstairs, so you might want to put some pants on."

"I'm pretty sure the good creamer is in this bed," Hunter said, rolling on top of me and attacking my neck until I dissolved into a fit of giggles.

"Get off me, you barbarian."

"Say the magic words," he said, holding my wrists above my head.

"Please?"

"No."

"Please get off me, Master Hunter?"

He considered that. "That's not bad."

"Please get off me, you sex fiend, and I promise to get *you* off later."

Hunter let go of my wrists. "I love how well you get me."

Laughing, I pushed him toward the edge of the bed until his feet hit the floor. Wrapping the blanket around me, I shuffled across the room and grabbed his pants from the floor before tossing them on the bed. Then I took a shift dress off the hanger and slid into a pair of flats. Yes, I own flats. I just rarely wear them. Short people need all the help they can get.

The kitchen lights were already on when we got downstairs. I glanced at the clock. Zoe must've just gotten in. And then speak of the damn devil. My right-hand woman stepped out of the walk-in freezer, and the expression on her face was priceless. She was slack-jawed and, for once, at a loss for words. But she wasn't looking at me. She was looking at the beddable specimen behind me.

Buuuusted. Oops.

"Morning, Zoe," I said, tucking my hair behind my ear. "We were just grabbing some coffee."

I reached for the full pot that I kept on a timer and took out two to-go cups. "Hunter, can you grab the creamer out of the refrigerator for me?"

"Sure thing."

As Hunter turned his back to us and opened the fridge to pull out the homemade mixture I kept in there, Zoe mouthed, *You whore.* I nodded proudly, and mouthed back, *I know.*

She made herself scarce as I poured two cups and handed one to Hunter. He boxed me in against the counter and kissed the side of my mouth. "Thank you," he said.

"Welcome. You sure you can't stay a little longer?"

"The guys might get suspicious if I work in a dress shirt."

"Good point." I wrapped my arms around him and his lips met mine again. "I've got to run errands today too, but I'll see you when I get back."

"Naked?"

Pushing him away with a laugh, I said, "All right, it's clear you've become addicted, so you need to get out."

"But I can *come* back later?"

"Oh sweet Jesus." I shoved him toward the front.

"Bye, Zoe," he called out over his shoulder.

"Bye, Hunter." She peered around the storage freezer and shook her head. "You have been a bad, bad girl, Ryleigh Phillips. But *that* is a hot piece of man meat even I could get behind."

LATER THAT MORNING, I rapped on the clear divider that separated Shayne's office from the rest of the open floor plan at HLS. She looked up from where it appeared she was playing a matching game with client photographs spread across her desk and smiled.

"Hey, what are you doing here?"

"I was in the neighborhood and thought I'd stop by," I said, tossing my purse into one of the seats in front of her desk.

Shayne's eyes were suspicious. "You're never just downtown during lunch hour."

I reached into my purse and held up a to-go bag. "I brought meat pies."

She gasped and reached over her desk to grab the bag. "You're a goddess and you can stop by any time. Did you remember the—"

"Extra tomato sauce? Yes, I did."

"And lamingtons! I love you, I love you, I love you," she said, whether to me or the decadent dessert in her hand, I wasn't sure.

Her phone rang then, and she shot daggers toward the front of the office. "Never hire someone who's incompetent about holding your calls during a meeting," she grumbled, setting the cake back in the bag before answering the phone in a sweet, peppy voice that betrayed what she was really thinking. After a few minutes of reassuring a client that she could indeed find someone who enjoyed gazing at and studying the planets as much as he did, she hung up and jotted something into a notebook, before looking up. "Oh bugger. Did he say astronomy or astrology?"

"Planets would be astronomy."

"That's it. Can you tell it's been a long morning?" She sighed and wrote the word "astronomy" into the book. "So you never said what's up."

"I just came by to ask if you could please tell your boss to stop booking dates for my boyfriend."

"Val? Of course, but—" Shayne jerked her head up as my words sank in. "Did you just say boyfriend?"

I couldn't hold back the massive grin that wanted to bust out any longer. "Yup."

"Fuck me dead. Are you serious? Wait," she said, eyeing me warily. "Which one?"

"Guess."

Her lips pursed as she studied me, and then she shook her head. "No way. No bloody way did you get the courage to choose Hunter."

"Oh yes I did. And he spent the night. *All* night."

"I'm so fucking proud of you!" She squealed and jumped up from her desk to squeeze me. "I was wondering when you'd come around to that conclusion."

"Come around? Why didn't you say something?"

She pulled back to look at me. "You didn't ask my opinion."

"Like that's stopped you from interfering before."

Shayne's hands went to her hips, and I realized then that she didn't seem as tall as usual today because she was barefoot. She was the complete opposite to me when it came to love of shoes. "You all sat me down two years ago and told me if I tried to matchmaker you up you'd deport me," she said.

"Aw, and our little hooker listened."

"Did you know it's because of you that Val only refers to me by that name now, even in public? She thinks it's a good tie-in with the company name."

"Hey, it's catchy."

"'Hooker, my meeting with the A-list celebrities has run a bit long, can you fetch my dry cleaning?'" she mimicked. "Or 'Could you be a good little hooker and stand outside the building with a sign advertising Hook, Line & Sinker, a fishing pole, and wearing a sexy mini? I think it'd really attract a new crowd to our services.'"

I bristled. "Sounds like you've got bigger problems to worry about than a nickname if she has you doing all that."

"That's not even the worst of it. Remind me to tell you about the hotel shit show over drinks later."

"You do know you're not her *assistant*, right? Does *she* remember that?"

Shayne waved her hand. "Enough about that. Let's talk about your news, please, because I'm dying for details."

As I filled her in on the events of the past few days, a Cheshire Cat grin spread across her face.

"Holy fuck," she said. "You're gonna get married and have ten kids and move to Burbank."

"Ew. Wait, he already lives in Burbank."

"See? It's happening."

I rolled my eyes. "I don't have time to roll out a

soccer team. I have to roll out a few dozen Licked chains first."

"Pshh. You've got that in the bag."

"I do *not*, but thank you for your vote of confidence."

"With Hunter helping you with the After Dark, it seems like it's a slam dunk. Good team professionally…good team in bed…"

"All right, all right. I'm going." I stood up and slung my purse over my arm, ready to bolt.

"Hmm. I wonder if Cameron would let me set him up," Shayne said, tapping her painted fingernail against her lips.

"You wouldn't."

"What? You said he was basically the ideal man *and* a sex god. And he's self-sacrificing. That's exactly what every woman in my client book is looking for." She scrunched her nose. "Sorry. Too soon?"

A flurry of activity could be heard from the front of the office, a woman's voice rising above all the others, and Shayne mumbled, "Look who's back from New York."

I didn't have to guess who she meant before Val thundered down the hall, heels stomping across the tiled floor. She didn't even spare a glance into Shayne's office as she passed.

"Oh, Val?" Shayne called out.

The footsteps stalled and then the clack of her heels could be heard as she stood in the doorway, overdressed in a tight leopard number with a brown fur wrap, even though it was over ninety degrees outside. There was a smirk on her painted red lips. "Is there something you need, Hooker? A coffee? A bib? An anal plug?"

To her credit, Shayne didn't even flinch. "Could you take Hunter Morgan off our books, please? As of today he's no longer listed as single."

"One night with a skanky brunette with money, and he's off the market?" Val clucked her tongue in disgust. "I was hoping to use him a bit more before some rich bitch tied him down. C'est la vie. Find me another hot cock."

"Actually, he's not with the girl you set him up with. He's with Ryleigh," Shayne said, gesturing to me.

Damn, I wish she hadn't done that.

Val's shrewd eyes looked me up and down. "Huh. Interesting choice if he likes the vintage sort." Then she let her fur wrap slide down her arms, leaving it trailing behind her as she turned and made her way to her office. "He as good in the sack as he looks?" she called over her shoulder, shutting her office door without waiting for a response.

Shayne gave me an apologetic smile. "Consider him off the record and all yours."

Be ready and hungry at five.

I CLOSED THE note Hunter had left for me on my dresser this morning and stuck it in my clutch. It'd been three days since he'd walk-of-shamed out of the Licked kitchen, and we'd been making the most of our free moments, which, with all the deadlines looming, hadn't been much. Tonight was going to be our first official date, and I couldn't wait to see what the surprise was.

The doorbell rang, and I fluffed my hair in the mirror, giving myself one last once-over. I'd chosen a black halter swing dress with a full skirt and red cherries all over it, and I'd left my hair down—yes, down—because Hunter seemed to like it that way best. After flipping off the lights, I bolted down the stairs and opened the outside door to see—

"Oh my God," I said, staring in awe at the man in front of me. "You're like my wet fantasy."

Hunter flashed a sexy smile and tossed his jacket over his shoulder. He was wearing black dress slacks, a short-sleeve white button-up with a black tie, and his hair was gelled back, fifties style. But the best part—oh heaven help me, the best part—was the Buddy Holly glasses he wore.

He cocked his head to the side, more of a James Dean move than a Buddy Holly one. "I thought for our first official date it should be something memorable."

"I think I need to change."

"No, you look great."

"I meant my panties."

Hunter laughed out loud. "I'll take that compliment, thank you."

"No," I said, taking his proffered arm, unable to stop looking at him. "Thank *you*."

"STILL NOT GONNA tell me where we're going?" I asked, tapping my toes in excitement as we sat at a red light.

"That would ruin the surprise. We're almost there anyway."

"Hmm. So somewhere in Hollywood where we're supposed to look out of this decade. Well, that could be anywhere around here." As he turned onto Highland, we hit a wall of traffic. "Oh wait a second. I know where we're going."

"Shoot."

"We're either going to your house, or…" I glanced at the hordes of people walking along the sidewalks with picnic baskets in hand and jumped up and down in my seat. "Are we going to the Hollywood Bowl?"

"It could be one of those two things," he said, nodding.

"It's totally the Bowl. Hell yes! I haven't been to a show here in forever. Who are we going to see? Or is it a theme night? Ooh, look, people are dressed up."

Hunter chuckled at my enthusiasm. "I'm glad you're excited."

"I'd be more excited if I knew what we were going to see," I singsonged.

"Patience is a virtue."

After parking the car in one of the packed lots—sandwiching it in, really—he grabbed a couple bags filled with food and drinks from the backseat, and then we made our way toward the entrance.

"Holy shit," I said when I saw the marquee proclaiming "Rock & Roll Sounds from the 50's & 60's" as the evening's theme. "This is so cool."

A group of men in T-Birds jackets and women in

Pink Ladies attire were posing for a picture in front of the sign, and when they were finished, Hunter asked if they'd take one of us. He handed his phone over then wrapped his arm around my waist, pulling me close as we smiled for the photo. Our photographer counted down from three, and when she said "one," Hunter grabbed me under my knees and lifted me into his arms. I laughed and yelped in surprise before reaching down to smooth my dress and make sure I wasn't flashing anyone.

"How was that one?" Hunter called out.

"So adorable," the woman said, handing his phone back.

And it was. She'd taken it at the exact moment he picked me up, huge grins on our faces, and my leg kicked up like I'd meant to do it. *Aww, our first photograph.* Yes, I'm aware that's sappy, but I just don't care.

As we walked up the incline, we passed event-goers picnicking everywhere—on blankets along every open spot of grass along the path and at picnic tables. So many of them sported doo-wop skirts and pedal pushers.

Ah. These were so my people.

"What do you think?" he asked, like he even needed to. This was so perfect for a first date that I couldn't even articulate it properly. Instead, I said, "You did good, Mr. Morgan. Really damn good."

Hunter led us to the garden boxes with a prime view of the stage, which was a bit of a surprise for me considering I'd never sat below section S way up high with the wooden bench seats before, but hey, I wasn't about to complain.

Our center box fit four people, but the other occupants hadn't arrived yet, so for a little while at least we had it all to ourselves. He set up the table and chairs before reaching into one of the bags he'd brought and pulling out a white tablecloth and a battery-powered candle.

"Ooh la la, you've gone all out tonight, haven't you?"

"Well," he said, looking up at me, "I really wanna get laid."

"No, you didn't just say that," I said as he laughed and went back to setting up. Making myself useful, I unpacked the bags, and—

"You brought Porto's! Shut up, shut up." I opened the familiar yellow box and feasted my eyes on the empanadas and potato balls lying inside. "How'd you know these were my favorite? And you brought the guava cheese things… Okay, now I'm drooling. I'm sorry, I know that's not sexy, but I'm so excited. How'd you know?"

"Hey, you told me before that I know everything about you, and now you doubt my ability to bring you food you like?" He tsked. "I hope you don't stroke out when you see the drinks."

"You have my full trust…at the moment."

When he was done, we took our seats, our own little private dinner party in the middle of the Bowl. The hills behind the amphitheater showcased a spectacular view, but it paled in comparison to the man in front of me.

And yes, he was still wearing the adorkable glasses.

"Just one more thing," he said, taking an insulated container out and pouring a slushy rose-colored beverage into our cups.

"No you didn't."

"I find it interesting that your favorite drink at Licked, according to Zoe, is called the Pink Pussy. Is there a story behind that I should know?"

Of course Zoe would say that. "Other than my love for strawberries, no," I said, holding up my cup as he did the same. "Well, there was that one time in college—"

"What?"

I gave him a wicked smile. "Just kidding. So what should we cheers to?"

Hunter held up his cup and thought about it for a minute. "To the possibility of last first dates."

"To last first dates," I repeated with a smile, clinking my drink against his and taking a long sip of the boozy strawberry shake. It wasn't *actually* my favorite at Licked, but then again, I didn't have a favorite. They were like my children; I couldn't choose.

He glanced down at the table and opened his palms wide. "So? What do you think?"

A smile spread across my lips and I shook my head. "I think you pretty much covered everything."

"Worthy of at least third base later?"

"Oh, I'd say you hit a home run. Feel free to cover *all* those bases."

Now, I'm not one of those girls who's shy about my

food. Not even on a date. They have to know what they're getting themselves into, in my opinion, otherwise you're stuck eating lettuce whenever you go out and gorging on everything in your kitchen when you get home. I'd already finished off seconds before I sat back from the table and patted my stomach. "That…was glorious."

"I have to say, for someone who's not a very daring eater, I was surprised to hear you liked Cuban food."

"Yeah, but Porto's is not weird food, it's an L.A. staple, thank you very much."

"Good point."

Glancing over at the still-empty chairs next to us, I gave him a curious look. "I'm surprised they're not taking advantage of this awesome box yet. Doesn't it start soon?"

Hunter just gave me a mischievous smile and shrugged.

"Did you…no. You wouldn't buy out two seats just to have the box to ourselves. Because that would be crazy."

"Yeah, that *would* be crazy."

My jaw dropped. "You are fucking insane, you know that?"

"I thought it was more along the romantic line, but I guess insane works too."

"That's too much," I said, shaking my head, but inside, I admit, there were hearts and flowers exploding everywhere.

"No. Never too much." His voice had dropped an octave. He held my gaze for a long moment before his eyes crinkled with amusement. "Besides. I never said I did it. Maybe they're just habitually late people."

I threw my napkin his way. "Or maybe you're just a liar who did an incredibly sweet gesture."

"Please don't tell your girlfriends. I don't need them giving me 'look at that poor sap' looks. Not yet, anyway."

"Nah, it would only throw them all into jealous rages. I'm not really in the mood to have to fend everyone off you." I caught a woman sitting in a row nearby glancing Hunter's way and laughed. "Okay, maybe it's a little too late for that."

"You do know I was carrying a big stick on our walk up here, right? I whacked a few guys who were wishing they had x-ray vision when you passed by."

"I must've missed that."

"I'm stealthy. It's a gift."

"I'll remember that in the future," I said, a smile tipping my lips.

"Excuse me, could I get a picture with you two?" came a woman's voice from behind us. She was dressed as Diana Ross, and her fellow Supremes were in long gold gowns behind her. "We've got to have a picture with our fellow musicians."

"Yeah, of course," I said, wondering what singer she thought I was. I pushed Hunter toward the middle so he could get a nice woman sandwich, and his hand went tight on my waist. After we'd posed for the photo, the Supremes wandered off, and in sync we heard them sing the chorus of

"Stop! In the Name of Love."

"Oh wow. Do I get a serenade from you too?" I asked, my fingers curling around Hunter's belt loops and pulling him closer. His arms went around me and his lips were warm on mine.

"You might get a private performance later if I feel you deserve it," he whispered in my ear.

Mmm. Consider me on my best behavior.

There was a steady stream of people stopping by our box and taking pictures of us in our outfits, though I was sure it was just so they could drool over Hunter later in the comfort of their sheets. But I couldn't blame them, nor did I mind. Who knew Buddy Holly was such a fox?

As the sun began to set, the band came out, each dressed in a full suit and tie, and one even wore glasses similar to Hunter's, which had him joking that "that asshole Buddy stole my look."

They put on an unbelievable rock 'n' roll concert with a stunning light show, infectious enthusiasm, and a wide range of hits. It was cool to hear some of my favorites live on stage instead of through the Licked speakers. We got a little Chuck Berry, a splash of Dion and the Belmonts, and, of course, plenty of Elvis. The only thing missing was a dance floor, but watching Hunter bop his head out of the corner of my eye to the music had a permanent smile on my face.

So…damn…hot. And mine. Did I mention that? Hands off, ladies.

No one else ever did show up in our box, so he'd set up a chair next to mine, his arm around the back as we enjoyed the show. Every now and again he'd sing along in my ear, and I couldn't help my surprise each time. He knew this world, knew the music, knew the acts, and it just eased something inside me. As I looked him up and down, I wondered if both of us had been born in the wrong decade. For so long I'd felt ostracized for the way I looked, for the things I liked. Then I'd been appeased by my closest friends and family, who'd accepted me for the everything-vintage, doo-wop-lovin' person I was, but I'd never actually felt like anyone understood and felt the same way. No one in my circle liked the same things I did, ice cream and boozy shakes not included.

But with Hunter's comforting presence next to me, it was like the missing piece I'd been searching for had finally snapped into place.

Oh geez. I've turned into a sappy ball of mush. You'll have to forgive me. I promise it won't happen too much, or even I might gag from the sugar.

Ahem.

When the band came back on stage for an encore, fireworks went off overhead, the most dazzling display of pyro lighting up the night sky. It gave me an idea for our Saturday Song Day menu—a rainbow confection called "The Peggy Sue" with Pop Rocks and a tiny pair of chocolate glasses on top. I needed to figure out how to make those, stat.

We stayed in our little safe haven as the rush filed out, nibbling on leftover empanadas. There was still a bit of the boozy shake left, and it gave me an idea for later in case his sweet tooth was as big as mine.

"So. You interested in staying for a nightcap?" I asked, my brow raised. "I know it'll be late when we get back, but—"

Hunter threw everything off the table into the bag before I finished my sentence and then tugged me out of the box toward the exit.

"Guess so," I said with a smirk.

GOTTA LOVE STACKED parking in L.A. Add that with the traffic, and we'd be sitting in his truck for a while.

"You're not tired, are you?" I said when I caught him stifling a yawn.

"Never."

"Hmm. I think you are. Maybe I should find some way to wake you up."

Hunter gave me a side-glance. "You have a caffeine drip I don't know about?"

"Well, no." I tapped the window with my finger. "These seem pretty tinted. I bet no one out there could see anything in here."

"I'd be surprised if they could." He narrowed his

eyes. "Why?"

Snuggling closer, I kissed his shoulder, working my way up his neck. "Because I don't like anyone to watch me eat my dessert."

I moved away and reached in the backseat for the bag that contained the remainder of the boozy shake. After taking the top off, I scooped some on my finger and sucked it into my mouth slowly.

Hunter's eyes didn't move from my mouth. "Do that again."

With a devious grin, I dipped my finger back inside and then painted my lower lip with the frozen strawberry mixture. "Want some?" I asked.

Still completely stopped in traffic, I leaned forward and waited for him to meet me the rest of the way. His eyes were hungry on my mouth, and he held my chin as his tongue came out to taste. Then he bit down on my lip before sucking it into his mouth.

"Fucking delicious," he said when he pulled away. A honk sounded behind him, and he inched the truck along at a snail's pace. Yeah, we'd be here for a while. And I, for one, was not complaining. I doubted he would be either in about thirty seconds.

"Looks like you need to keep your eyes on the road, mister," I said, nibbling his ear as I pulled his shirt out of his pants and unfastened the bottom buttons. "But don't worry. I'll make sure you get your dessert too."

A low rumble came from his chest. "I think you're

trouble."

The belt he was wearing came off, and the zipper went down. "I think you may be right."

When my fingers curled under the band of his pants, he lifted his hips and I pushed them, along with his boxer briefs, down his thighs. He was already getting hard, his cock just waiting to get licked, and I was more than happy to oblige. I leaned down over him, flicking my tongue over the tip, and felt him tense.

That. That reaction is powerful. Knowing you're in control of someone's pleasure, that your mouth has the ability to get them off and make their wildest fantasies come true—*that* is hot as hell.

His reaction had me moving my mouth down over his length, the feel of him warm and firm on my tongue. He truly was the best thing I'd ever tasted—I doubted anything I tried to replicate would come close to matching the taste that was all Hunter.

"Fuuuuck," he said, arching up into my mouth. "You're gonna make me wreck the fucking truck with that mouth."

I lifted my head. "I can stop," I teased.

"No, no, let's not get crazy. Where you going? Come back," he said, reaching for me. I took the canister of Pink Pussy out of the cup holder. I'd really have to rename the drink after I'd had it all over Hunter's impressive cock.

Pouring some of the drink into my mouth, I leaned over his lap again and slowly sucked him inside, a tiny bit of the liquid escaping my lips and dripping down his erection.

When I swallowed, I heard a strangled "God, Ryleigh," and one of his hands fisted through my hair. He was white-knuckling the steering wheel with his other hand, his breaths coming out ragged.

I stuck my fingers in the canister, getting them nice and covered, and then I let the drops fall down onto his tanned lower stomach and over the tip of him. He sucked in a breath, whether from the cold milkshake or from anticipation, I didn't know. His hand tightened on my hair, holding it out of my face as I lifted my head from his throbbing length and planted kisses along the path from his abs down his pelvis.

"You are seriously…testing…my self-restraint," he said, his voice full of grit.

When I moaned in agreement around his cock, I felt it jerk, his rock-solid erection ready to combust.

His jaw was clenched and he kept his eyes straight ahead, not wanting to give away what was happening should the windows turn out to be not quite as private as we hoped they were.

We were moving, albeit very slowly, and I was thankful we were in a truck a bit higher off the ground than my little Mini. Not that I would've cared about an audience at this point—there was no way I was stopping until we were both completely satisfied.

"Fuck…feels…so good…fuck."

More drizzle. More teasing with my tongue. My lips

tightened as I went down again, my fingers lightly caressing his balls, causing a guttural moan to rise out of his throat.

"Gonna…come," he warned, but I kept my mouth right where it was. Then his body tensed and jerked, his orgasm coming in a white-hot rush down my throat. I sucked down every last drop of him, the taste of strawberries still strong in my mouth.

When he was finished, I leaned down again, my tongue coming out to catch any sweetness I'd missed. He let out a shuddering breath, his hand easing off my head as I sat up.

"Yummy," I said, giving him a devilish look as I cleaned my fingers off one by one with my mouth.

"Christ, woman." Hunter shook his head and pulled his pants back up. "You're in so much trouble when we stop."

"Oh? But I wasn't done yet." Sliding my panties down my legs, I took them off and then tossed them into one of the bags in the back. I reclined the seat a little and threw my left leg over the console so that my ankle rested in his lap, opening myself wide.

Keeping my eyes on the sexy man next to me, I inched up my dress to my waist, leaving me completely exposed as Hunter hit the gas, the traffic finally dissipating.

"Ryleigh…fuck."

Getting him off, knowing anyone could see us, had made me wet and needy, my body aching for a sweet release. I teased my thighs with my fingertips, watching him continue to peer over at me while trying to focus on the road. When I touched myself, he cursed again, one of his hands coming off the steering wheel and across the seat, but I swatted him away.

"You get to touch all you want…soon. If you can get us back to my place in one piece."

He growled, a feral sound that had me growing wetter. My fingers slid between my lower lips, and then back up to focus on my clit. I circled it, increasing the pressure as my breath hitched, and a spasm of pleasure shot down the lower half of my body.

I moaned Hunter's name, and this time I let him touch me when he reached for me again. His large palm covered mine at first, following my movements as I undulated against our hands. Then he moved his lower, coating himself in my juices before sliding a thick finger inside me. I cursed, throwing my head back against the seat and stroking my clit again. How he kept his eyes on the road and drove in a straight line while I rocked against his hand, I had no idea, but it just proved how much control he had. I doubted I'd have as much.

"Another," I said on a gasp, and he obeyed, filling me with a second digit. I rode his fingers as he flew down the road, trying to draw out the pleasure as long as I could, barely noticing when we'd arrived.

Hunter slammed on the brakes, put the car in park, and shut it off before moving across the seat and leaning down to put his mouth between my legs. His tongue thrust inside me, wild and voracious, as if he'd been starving and I was the best thing he'd tasted in years. I grabbed the back of his head, my legs shaking and my eyes slamming shut as the pressure swelled, my body tightening all over before exploding in a release that had me both lightheaded and panting out his name.

"Oh my…" I tried to say, taking a deep breath. "That was…damn."

Hunter took one last lick and then he gazed up at me, his eyes still heavy with lust. Then he gave me a look that was full of mischief.

"I believe you just…what's the term you use? Got Licked."

A WEEK LATER and it was chaos. Utter chaos.

The shop was in the busiest part of the season, never an empty booth in sight, Hunter's team was in the final stages of priming everything, the furniture was slowly being delivered and then subsequently covered in plastic, *and* the producers of *Wake Up America* were due to stop by to check out the space, oh, anytime now.

Stressed didn't even begin to cover it.

"Has anyone seen my clipboard?" I asked, frantically searching, opening and shutting drawers, lifting bowls off the counter.

"I don't think it's in the freezer, boss," Zoe said, shaking her head. "Maybe you could go in there and chill out for a bit, though."

I shut the freezer door. "Aren't you a comedian. They'll be here any minute and I've got all my stuff organized on it. I even color-coded with highlighters."

"This is why you should switch to computers. I've told you this."

"Ugh. Computers schmuters," I said, collapsing on top of the counter and banging my head against the cold stainless steel.

"Am I interrupting something?" a deep, familiar voice asked, and my head shot up. Hunter had peeked his head around the corner and was looking at me with an amused expression.

"My clipboard's not in the freezer. I'm toast."

Zoe gave him a pat on the shoulder. "She's all yours."

"Find my highlights or you're fired," I called out. "Fired, I say."

"What's missing?" he asked, coming into the room.

Sighing dramatically, I pulled myself off the counter. "The release forms I signed for the show, among other things. I had them on the clipboard I always keep in the drawer, and it's not there." My arms went around his neck and I gave him my best pout. "Help?"

"I must've missed the 'please' in there somewhere," he said, one hand going around my waist.

"Please, *please* help me, you big strong man you." Yes, I said all that with a straight face, but trust me, it wasn't easy.

"You say you searched everywhere?"

"Up and down and all around."

"Hmm." He leaned down and gave me a kiss but then pulled back. "Did you say it was on a clipboard? Huh. That's funny."

"No, it's not funny. Don't make me fire you too."

"Well I just so happened to stumble across this hiding behind the bar next door," he said, pulling my clipboard from behind his back.

"Oh my God, you found it. I love you, I love you, I love you." I hugged the clipboard to my chest and gave a happy squeal. And then I realized what the hell I'd just said.

My eyes went wide and I knew I had to have flushed seven shades of purple. Oh yes. My skin definitely bypassed the pink flush and went straight to head-about-to-pop-off purple. Gulping, I said, "Uh…I didn't mean that the way it sounded. Like, the love part. I would've said, I like you, I like you, I like you, but it doesn't really flow as well, huh?"

He laughed and planted a kiss on the top of my head. "I know what you meant, silly girl."

Zoe strode into the kitchen again, her thumb pointing back toward the shop. "It's go time. Aw, and look, your hot piece of ass found what you were looking for." She clapped Hunter on the back. "Good job, boy toy."

I took a big inhale and then blew it out in a rush. They were here. And I was a professional about to blow them away. *Yes. Good. Awesome pep talk.*

Hunter ran his hands up and down my arms. "Kick some ass, Miss Phillips."

Nodding, I pulled away and looked over my clipboard, making sure all was in order. "All right. I'm doing this."

"Good luck," they said in unison.

Even though I'd met with them before when I'd won a spot on the show, I knew anything could happen and I still needed to bring my A-game. I wiped my sweaty hands off on my pencil skirt and lifted my chin before walking out to the front.

"Mr. Lieberman. Ms. Watts." I gave them firm handshakes and we said our hellos, and then they moved aside to introduce me to their lighting director, Tony.

"Thank you so much for coming by," I said. "I reserved a booth for us, but first, may I interest you in trying out one of our sundaes or shakes?"

"Ooh, I'd love to try one," Mr. Lieberman said. "I think I remember one with cheesecake ice cream, do you still have that?"

"Cheesecake ice cream with Oreo, crumbled graham cracker crust, and fudge? We sure do," I told him.

"Perfect," he said, rubbing his hand over his suit-clad stomach.

"And for you two?" I asked.

"Chocolate, chocolate, and more chocolate sounds good to me," Tony said.

Ms. Watts pursed her lips. "I usually like something

a bit more…outside the box, if you know what I'm saying. Not so generic."

That felt like a slap at me, but I put a smile on my face anyway and said, "We've got a sweet corn ice cream with raspberry swirl that I think would be right up your alley."

"Sweet corn," she murmured, tapping her chin. "I suppose that'll do."

"Great. If you'll have a seat at the reserved table right over there, I'll place our orders and be right with you."

Then I walked over to the counter to Zoe and gave her the rundown.

"Got it," she said. "Go kill it."

"Will do. Oh, and Z?"

"Yeah, boss?"

"Make sure when you bring out the desserts, you say the names of them with extra oomph. I think they'd really like that." I winked, and when I turned, I saw Hunter in the doorway, the tarp lifted a few inches so he could see what was going on.

You got this, he mouthed, and I smiled, grateful for his encouragement. Had it really only been a few short weeks that he'd been in my life? It felt as though he was the one I'd known since high school, not Cameron. How was that even possible?

"So Miss Phillips—" Mr. Lieberman started.

"Ryleigh, please."

He gave me a friendly smile. "Ryleigh. The first

order of business before we go any further would be to go over the contracts and make sure we've all signed off on them. Do you have any questions for us before you do that?"

"No, I've looked over them with my lawyer and they look great," I said, handing the original signed forms his way. I had three extra copies for me too because, well, you can never have enough copies, right?

"Perfect." He flipped through the pages and signed off on each one before passing them to Ms. Watts.

"Now, Ryleigh, we'd like to go over again how the process will work and what you can expect the day of the show. First, remember that only the winner determined by audience votes and judge's scores will walk away with the cash prize and the backing to open at least five chain stores in major cities around the country."

"Yes, sir, I'm on board with that."

"Good. Now, Tony here is in charge of all the lighting and getting it set for the film crew to come in and do their thing. They'll be here to set up around two thirty that afternoon, but no later than three. We'll begin your interview around six thirty, after we've gotten some shots of the interior and exterior. Also, if you could also have a staff member or two on hand that day, that'd be great. We'll want shots of the drinks and food, but we'll have to be quick before it all melts."

"Speaking of melting," Zoe said in a projected voice as she came up to the table, a tray in hand. "I've got a Triple Nipple Fudge, a Stroke 'n Poke, and a Clam Jam for you fine folks."

I helped place the desserts in front of each of them and thanked Zoe before inviting them to dig in.

Ms. Watts stared at her sundae, gorgeously drizzled with a raspberry sauce to die for, and prodded it with her spoon. "Which name is this?" she asked, wrinkling her nose.

"That would be the Clam Jam, ma'am," I said with a smile.

She jerked her head up at me and then looked back at the bowl in front of her. "The…right."

"This might be the most heavenly thing I've ever put in my mouth," Mr. Lieberman said. "Stroke 'n Poke. That's hilarious."

"It's obscene, is what it is," the blond woman said in a hushed voice. "What about the kids who come to this store?"

I looked around at the customers and shrugged. "I don't see any kids here, and we don't get a lot of them anyway with the warning sign outside the front door and all. The ones who do come usually just get a Dirty Smurf, and they think it's cute that it's named after a cartoon."

Mr. Lieberman laughed at that. "I'll have to bring my son here sometime, then."

His coworker was not amused.

As they ate their sundaes—and yes, even Miss Stick in the Mud ate a large dent of hers—I refreshed them on how Licked functioned, how the After Dark would run once it opened, what my plan was for the (possible) future chains, and what my business numbers over the past two years since we'd been opened looked like. And all this using my—woohoo—handy-dandy color-coded notes.

Mr. Lieberman set down his spoon when he'd finished and said, "I must say, it's impressive that a woman your age is bringing in those kinds of numbers after such a short period of time. Most would still be in the red, and those are people much older than you. Not to mention the concept is original, the desserts are topnotch, and the design"—he glanced around the room—"well, it's just fantastic. What's your experience prior to this?"

I beamed. "Thank you, I appreciate that. I learned a lot from working in my grandparents' ice creamery during summers when I was younger, and then when I graduated I was there full-time until they retired. I'm not sure I could handle the business side if it weren't for them. They also invested in my idea, and that's the only reason I even have a business to call my own."

"You're lucky," the woman said.

"Or hardworking," her partner chimed in.

She pushed her sundae away. "May we see the bar portion of your business now?"

"Of course. Right this way." I led them over to the entrance and lifted the tarp so the trio could pass through. As they entered, Ms. Watts let out an "Oh…oh my."

Clearing my throat, I motioned at Hunter's guys busy at work. "As you can see, we're still in the middle of piecing together the final touches and moving in the furniture, but we'll be ready by the day of the show. The booths will be set along the wall opposite the bar, and we'll have an assortment of high-tops scattered throughout the area. There will also be a back lounge, which I explained a bit about earlier."

Ms. Watts eyed the plastic-covered tables with a pointed brow. "I must admit, I'm a little surprised everything is still in such disorder. Yours is the only one we've seen that isn't ready to go, isn't that right, Jim?"

"That's true, Kathy," Mr. Lieberman answered, "but I'm sure there's some logical explanation."

They all looked at me expectantly.

Shit. Shit fucker on a stick. I racked my brain trying to find something polite to say, besides the *Hunter and his team have been busting their asses, so would you kindly fuck off?* that wanted to fly out.

But that's not what came out of my mouth. Instead, I said, "I had a few setbacks with the original construction team, but not to worry. These guys will have everything up and running well before the day of filming." Then I gave them a confident smile.

Ms. Watts sniffed. "We surely hope so, or we can't promise things will go well for you."

"Meaning?"

"Well, we're still contracted to have you *tape* the show, but that doesn't mean we have to air your segment if things are"—she looked around at the flurry of workers—"still in disarray."

Oh my Jesus. Stay cool. Don't grab that hammer and chase her down with it.

"I can assure you it won't come to that," I said, finding it harder to keep a pleasant expression on my face this time. I wasn't worried we wouldn't make the deadline, but I *was* worried now that they had it out for me. *Big fat fucking fuck.*

They walked through the space, Tony taking notes and measuring for the setup. The crew working stayed silent and inconspicuous while the trio browsed, and Hunter gave me a wink when we passed.

"Well, Ryleigh, we look forward to seeing you in two weeks," Mr. Lieberman said, extending his hand to shake mine. "I can't wait to see what you do with this place."

"Thank you sir. Ma'am. Tony." I waved at them as they went out the door of the After Dark, and then pressed the heels of my hands over my eyes. "Oh my God, oh my God, oh my God."

"That woman was a cunt," T said, standing on the ladder and waving his paintbrush in her direction. "You should name an ice cream after her."

"I've got one. It's called the Who's Afraid of the Big, Bad Bitch."

"I like it," T said with a laugh as Hunter walked up and rubbed my shoulders.

"You know we've got this," he told me. "Don't stress about her. Once they see what you've put together, there'll be no denying you should be on that show."

"She hates me already. You should've seen her face when I told her the ice cream she ordered was called the Clam Jam."

He laughed. "Remind me to try that one later."

"Later, you say?" I asked, perking up.

"Get your head out of my pants, Phillips."

"Now why would I ever do such a stupid thing?"

He shook my shoulders. "Listen. This is you. She may not get that, but this business…Licked and the After Dark…it has everything you are spilled into it. You're gonna kill it, trust me. My only worry is that once it airs I'll never see you again because of the stampede."

"Well, I have to make sacrifices for my adoring fans, what can I say? I promise to pencil you in at least twice a week."

"You hear this?" Hunter asked T. "Give a woman what she wants and she tosses you out like yesterday's trash." He shook his head. "Women."

I fingered the paint-splattered coveralls he was wearing today, proof positive that Hunter could look hot in any damn thing.

"Maybe I'll let you stick around if you wear these later," I said, my voice low so only he could hear.

"Maybe you should let me try some of that Clam Jam now, hmm?"

"That could be arranged." I pulled him by his overalls and headed back under the tarp.

"I heard all that," T called after us, shaking his head. "Perverts."

Chapter Twenty

The Real You

I WAS FLIPPING through our Ballot Box of Assholes when Paige strolled through the front door the next day. I know what you're thinking: About time that feisty blond broad made a return.

Wait, that's not what you're thinking? Ohhh, you're probably wondering about the Ballot Box of Assholes. I don't mean to brag, but it's only one of the greatest things ever. It's a suggestion box where customers can enter their horror stories featuring an asshole ex, asshole roommate, asshole teacher… Well, you get the picture.

Each week I choose an entry, put together a sundae or shake combination, and then give it a super-sweet name. The person whose story I choose can also come in and get the dessert for free as many times as they want throughout the week it's featured. For example, the one this week was a rum shake inspired by a cheating bastard with a pirate fetish. I called it: "I Hope It Shrivels Up and Falls Off."

Classy, right?

"Ooh pick mine, pick mine," Paige said, coming up behind me and eyeing the slips of paper in my hand. "If you see one about a bridezilla named Tammy, go with that one. Although I guess it's enough that karma smacked that bitch with a case of the herps."

I snort-laughed and glanced at her over my shoulder. "What? How do you even know that?"

"I got curious-slash-annoyed after she made me move her wedding date *and* they postponed the honeymoon plans I'd helped swing. Super last minute. Super chaos for me. Anyway, I fed her maid of honor some vodka for dinner one night and it all came spilling out."

Laughing harder, I shoved the entries into a manila folder and turned to face my psychotic friend. "There's no one in this world quite like you, you know that?"

"Thank fuck. One of a kind over here."

"Isn't that the truth. You hungry? Thirsty? Oh, hey, can you try this and tell me what you think?" I called one of my staff over to bring me a sample of the new flavor I'd made this morning. All new ideas were tested on the floor, and I currently had Heather making the rounds to customers and getting feedback.

"What is it?" Paige sniffed the ice cream. "It smells

like watermelon."

"That's because it's the new one I'm thinking about putting out for our Friday night, 'Flavors from Your Favorite Flicks' theme. You get one guess as to what I'm calling that one. Think movie lines."

She took a bite with the tiny wooden spoon and her eyes drifted shut. "Mmm, so fucking yum. I'm gonna go with 'I Carried a Watermelon.'"

"Wow. I'm impressed," I said, shaking my head. "Maybe I should have you naming these instead. Whaddya say? Quit that whole wedding shtick and come up with naughty ice cream all day?"

"Tempting, but my job is way too entertaining to give up."

"I was hoping you'd say that. It'd break my heart to lose all the juicy gossip."

"Mine too," she said, finishing off her ice cream. Then she nodded next door. "I don't hear chainsaws or whatever the hell has been going on over there. They still working?"

"Yeah, but they're almost done. I need to check with Hunter to see if it's still okay to help out tomorrow."

"Uh…help out like manual labor? Why would you do that to yourself when you're paying someone else to deal with the hassle?"

I shrugged. "I just thought maybe I should contribute a bit. Nothing major, obviously, I don't wanna mess anything up."

"If you insist. But speaking of that hot man," she said, rubbing her hands together, "how's it going?"

"Good…like, insanely good. I'm trying not to jinx anything over here, but…" I bit my lip.

"But what? Spit it out, Ry. Are you trying to tell me I'll be planning your wedding sometime soon? Better book me now."

"No," I said quickly. "I mean, it's still too soon to think about anything like that. That'd be insane."

"But you've thought about it." Not a question.

"Doesn't every girl think about it?"

"Hell no," Paige said, scrunching her nose. "Actually, that's not true. Most do that whole scribbling their names together with hearts all over a notebook thing. I never have, but that's also because I don't plan to get married."

"I hope you're not blasting that info out to your clients."

"Trust me when I say they're so busy talking about themselves, their perfect wedding, and how amaaaazing their groom is that my love life isn't even a blip on their radar." She held up her ring finger and flashed a platinum band of diamonds she'd bought for herself after her first big event. "Plus, I keep this on, and they assume I'm married and in a perpetual state of bliss. Now are you going to show me the new place or do I have to beg?"

"You have to beg."

"Ugh. For fuck's sake." Paige started to get down on

her knees, and I laughed and pulled her back up.

"Come on, ya wacko." Lifting the edge of the tarp, we walked into the not-so-disaster-anymore area. It was coming along so well; the construction was finished, the first stages of paint were being applied, and then it was time for the fun part—the decorating part.

"Ta-da," I said when we entered.

Paige's jaw fell open as she walked around, her steps careful on the plastic covering the floor from any splatters. "Holy shit. You have a bar. A super-kickass-looking bar. Can I live here?"

"Sure, I'll put a bed in the back."

"Make it one of those circular rotating ones."

"Nothing but the best for you, my dear." I caught T's eye from where he was working on the wall behind the bar.

"Hey hey," he said, coming over to the end. "How's it lookin'?"

"Unbelievable. Really. I can't believe you've gotten so much done in just a few short weeks. I'm blown away."

"Glad you approve," he said, giving me a pleased smile.

I looked around for that disheveled head of hair, but I didn't see him anywhere.

"Hey, is Hunter around?" I asked.

"No, it's Tuesday."

"So?"

"He always runs out for a couple hours every Tuesday and Thursday."

He did? "Runs out where exactly?"

T looked wary, as if he wondered if maybe he'd said too much. "Uh…I'm not sure. Personal business. But he's always on the job early those days or stays later."

Huh. Making up the hours wasn't the issue. I cared about what was so important he left twice a week to do it. Come to think of it, there had been a couple times where I'd stopped by and he'd been out. I'd just assumed he'd gone for supplies or something, but now that T had confirmed this was something routine for him, it had my curiosity piqued. *Whatever it is, it's not anything he's shared with me.* Yeah, that bothered me more than I wanted to admit, though we were still in that whole getting-to-know-you phase, so it wasn't like I could expect him to spill everything yet.

Still…

"Want me to tell him to stop by when he gets back?" T asked as he edged away, clearly ready to get back to work to avoid saying something that would get him in trouble.

"No…no, that's okay. Not a big deal." I gave T a tight smile before Paige and I walked back over to Licked.

"What the hell was that about?" Paige asked, her brow raised. "Sounds like some booty-call shit to me."

I gave her the finger.

"I'm serious," she said. "He skips out twice a week to go somewhere and you didn't have a clue about it?"

"It's not like I've asked him."

"It's not like you *knew* to ask him."

"Paige…"

"Sketchy," she said, shaking her head. "We should follow him next time."

"What? I'm not following him. I'll just ask him about it later."

Paige crossed her arms. "If he hasn't told you anything yet, I bet he lies. Or gets all defensive. If he does, we are *so* spying."

"It won't come to that. I'm sure he hasn't thought to bring it up because it's no big deal."

"Or it's a *big* deal and he's hiding it."

I groaned. "What do I have to do to shut you up?"

"Get me another one of those watermelon things. But drown it in booze this time."

"WHAT DO YOU think?" Hunter asked the next morning when he'd opened the gallon canister of paint I'd be using. He stirred the contents with a wooden stick and then glanced up at me. "Vibrant enough for you?"

"Well, I was hoping for neon and glow in the dark, but it'll have to do," I joked. "It's gonna look so great."

"I think so too. Would you mind grabbing a couple of those one-inch brushes over there?" He nodded at the tools and supplies in the corner of the back lounge where I'd be getting my paint on.

I picked up two of the brushes he'd indicated, and

crouched down next to him as he poured the paint into the tray. He'd made me wear a pair of beige coveralls today, which I was positive I looked stunning in—*hah*—and I'd traded in my heels for sneakers I'd found in the back of my closet. Waaaay in the back. Still, I was rather excited about the prospect of getting my hands dirty.

"So how do we do this, exactly?" I asked.

"What, paint?"

"Yes, paint. I've never done this before, so which way do I stroke it?"

A smirk appeared on Hunter's face. "You're asking me how you should stroke it."

"That's what I said. I don't want to mess it—" Then it occurred to me what he was implying, the cheeky bastard. "Strokes. Paint strokes. Ass."

"Need me to show you how to wax on, wax off, do I, Ryleigh-san?" It looked as though he was trying to hold back a laugh, but he was losing that battle.

"Fine. Maybe T could show me," I said, getting to my feet to head to the front where the rest of the guys were working, but Hunter reached for my arm before I could get far and tugged me back.

"Don't even fucking think about it." He held my chin and gave me a kiss that had my insides melting. *And holy damn, the man could kiss.* I felt bad for the rest of the population that would never experience the taste of him.

Actually, no I didn't. I was greedy like that.

When he let me go, I licked my lips. "You're very

convincing."

"Sometimes. Here, hold this," he said, putting the brush in my hand and covering it with his own. Then he dipped the tip inside the orchid paint and leaned us in closer to the table we had lying on its side so we could paint the underside first. He held our hands at the top of it and then brushed them down in one long motion. We repeated the move again, and then he kissed me under the ear.

"And that's how you stroke it," he said with an impish grin. "Any questions?"

"If that's all there is to it, I think I can take it from here."

"No doubt in my mind." He stood up and reached for the extended roller brush he'd set out, plunging it in his own paint tray before starting on the wall. I couldn't help but watch him work, loving the way the fit of his white t-shirt molded to his back as he pushed the roller up and down. Loved the way every few minutes his head would jerk to the side as he flicked his hair off his forehead. And I *especially* loved knowing what was underneath all those clothes.

"You watching me paint or watching my ass?" Hunter asked, still facing away from me. *Damn,* I must be transparent if he could guess that.

"Your ass. Always."

He laughed, turning around to immerse the roller in the tray again. His brown eyes crinkled in amusement, but hidden inside their dark depths was a bit of something akin to satisfaction and…lust.

Don't get me wrong, I loved when he looked at me that way. It had my heart pumping and my thighs tingling, and it made me want to pinch myself. It just *also* made what I needed to ask harder to broach.

Deciding to concentrate instead on the movement of my brush up and down the table, I said, "I, uh…came over here yesterday to show Paige around and check about the paint stuff for today, but T said you'd stepped out."

"Oh. Sorry I missed you."

"No big deal, it wasn't important. Is everything okay?"

"Yeah, everything's good." He continued painting the wall.

"Okay," I said, trying to figure out a way to get him to give me more details, since he wasn't offering anything up. I wasn't about to throw T under the bus and ask why he disappeared twice a week without explanation. "Did you have to pick up more supplies?"

"What?" He looked over his shoulder. "No, we've got everything covered. Could you toss me the red edger next to you?"

"This thing?" I asked, holding up something rectangular.

"Yep, thanks."

Picking up my brush again, I dipped it in the paint and made smooth strokes along the leg of the table. I couldn't understand why he wasn't being more forthcoming, but maybe I just had to come out and say it. It wasn't like we needed to hide anything from each other. *Right?*

"Can I ask you something?"

"Sure," he said.

"Where do you go?" When he stopped his movements and looked over his shoulder, I continued, "I've noticed you leave for a few hours a couple times a week, and I was just wondering…how come?"

Hunter dropped his gaze, the roller twisting in his hand as if he was weighing what he wanted to say. Then he shook his head slightly. "Just some appointments I couldn't miss. I come in early those days, if that's what you're—"

I held up my hand. "No, that's not an issue. I was just curious, is all."

He stared at me, more behind his eyes than what he was saying, but the only response I got was "Okay." Then he dipped his roller in the tray again and went back to work while I sat there watching him.

Was it something bad? He said appointments…did he mean medical ones? Was he sick? Dying? Ugh, no, I did not need that popping into my head. All those damn Nicholas Sparks-type books were rubbing off on me. You know, the ones where the romance is going great and then boom—HEA turned ugly-cry-fest.

Maybe Paige was right. Could it be something he was deliberately hiding? I didn't believe Hunter was the cheating type, but I wasn't stupid enough to believe any guy under the right circumstances wouldn't. He was certainly gorgeous enough, and Lord knew I'd thought he was a ladies' man before we'd started dating.

He'd tell me when he was ready to. *Right?* Right.

"THIS WAS A stupid decision. Turn around." I slumped down in the passenger seat of Paige's car and covered my face with my hands.

"You need answers, and we're gonna get 'em. Now put your damn wig on."

I fingered the short bubblegum-pink bob in my hands and wondered again why I'd decided following Hunter today—and involving my bad-influence friend—was a good idea.

It was Thursday afternoon, and after picking me up a few blocks down from Licked, Paige and I were trailing my boyfriend as his truck weaved through L.A. on the way to his weekly "appointment."

Paige glanced my way, her own hair hiding underneath long blue locks. Yeah, we didn't look inconspicuous at all.

"You said he gave you the runaround trying to avoid the question. Now you can't stop wondering what it could be, so after today, we'll know."

Sighing, I put on the wig, not happy about my lack of

faith.

Yes, I was aware how this could monumentally blow up in my face, but if…and see, that was the other option. The "but if" one where it *could* be something notsogood, and didn't I have a right to know? Still, my stomach felt queasy.

"Why do you even have these anyway? Did you get them at a stripper sale?"

"Role play," Paige said, making a left onto a side street.

"I'm sorry I asked."

"Hey, look, he's turning." She pulled the car off to the side of the road, close enough that we could still see but far enough away he wouldn't notice. "Wait…are we at an—"

"Elementary school," I said. "Uh…yeah, we are." *What…the hell…*

"He has kids?"

"I didn't think so."

"Maybe he's picking up a niece or nephew or something."

I couldn't take my eyes off him as he parked and went around the school to the back, where I could see a bunch of kids running around on a playground. "No, his family all live in Chicago."

"Oh fuck."

We stayed silent, my heart beating loudly in my chest, as he reemerged a few minutes later, this time with a little girl by his side. She couldn't be older than six or so, with long chestnut hair pulled up in two pigtails, and a sweet smile aimed up at Hunter.

My chest clenched. He had a kid? That was what he didn't want to tell me? But why? I wasn't anti-children. Hell, I loved them…most of the time.

The girl stumbled, but Hunter caught her in time, and then he crouched down to tie the loose laces of her shoe. She nodded at whatever he was saying to her, and then he kissed her forehead and took her book bag for her. Grabbing her hand, he stopped at the edge of the sidewalk and had her look both ways before crossing to his truck.

Their affection was apparent, and it had me melting a little. Hunter with a kid was the sweetest thing I'd ever seen. I wished he'd told me about it, but I couldn't blame him for not saying anything. Although…he'd been spending most of his nights with me lately, as well as working during the day. When did he have her other than these two days a week? I shook the thought out of my head. I had no room to judge as it was, seeing that I was his untrusting girlfriend stalker. But I was ready to give him back his privacy. It had been wrong for me to come here.

"Can we go now?" I asked Paige, and she started the car back up before U-turning away from the school.

Pulling off my wig, I watched in the side mirror as his truck grew smaller in the distance. Hunter wasn't who I'd thought he was at all when I'd first met him. And it occurred to me then that I'd judged him by his appearance and assumed the same way I'd hated people doing the same to me all these years.

Life. It was ironic at the best of times.

I'D TRIED TO wait for Hunter to open up to me. Really, I had. But after a full twenty-eight and a half hours of having the images of him and who I assumed was his daughter playing on a loop in my mind, my curiosity was winning out. I knew it was time to say something when I was still thinking about it even as he kissed me with my arms pinned over my head against the wall.

Which was where we currently were.

"I think we should play a game," I said as he cupped my breast over my clothes, his mouth gently nibbling down my neck. Yes, this wasn't the ideal time to bring it up, but I couldn't focus on how good everything felt when my head was a million miles away. Hell, you know we females never have the best timing with these kinds of things—gimme a break.

"I ask you a question, you answer, and then I'll lose an item of clothing. And vice versa," I said.

"Or I could just get us naked right now instead." He pushed me onto my bed and then raised his shirt up over his head. Okay, so this was a distracting view…a *really* distracting view…

Focus. Ask him questions. Make him talk.

"Is there anything you want to know about me?" I asked, sitting up on my hands as he walked toward me, my eyes going again to his ripped abs.

"Are you asking me to play twenty questions right now? Seriously?"

"I need to know more about the guy taking up so much of my time."

"In bed," he said with a sexy grin as he climbed onto the bed, pushing me down to the mattress, his body covering mine. He sucked my bottom lip into his mouth, and I moaned, half out of pleasure, half out of frustration. He was way too good at taking my mind off everything but him.

"Question one," I said, before things could go any further. His lips were on my neck, leaving a hot trail of kisses, and it wouldn't be long until he rendered me completely useless.

"You're not really quizzing me while I do this, are you?" he said, as his mouth made its way over my collarbone. Then he lifted his head, an indecent promise in his eyes. Tempting, *oh so tempting*. But I was determined to make him talk to me.

"What can I say? I'm a multitasker."

He groaned then pulled the top of my strapless dress down over my chest. "Fine. My question is, do you like it when I do this?" He flicked his tongue over my nipple, and I gasped, my fingers spearing through his hair.

Oh, fuck, he doesn't play fair.

"Yes," I said, squirming underneath him. "I love that and you should feel free to do it whenever you like. But that's not a good question."

"It's all you're getting out of me at the moment."

"Okay, I'll go. Do you have kids?"

His face nuzzled my breast as he inched my dress down to my waist. "Not that I know of."

Wrong answer. "Are you sure?"

He lifted his head, chuckling. "I'm pretty sure I'd know."

Okay, if he's not gonna fess up to the kid thing, I'm busting out the big guns. "Where do you go on Tuesdays and Thursdays?"

His body went still for a moment, and then his lips were warm on my stomach. "Come on, I don't wanna talk about this right now."

"Well, I do."

"Ryleigh—"

"Please?"

Sighing, he rolled off me onto his back. "I told you I had appointments. I don't know why you can't just leave it at that."

"Because it feels like you're hiding something."

"Should I give you a calendar of everywhere I'll be? Is that how relationships work? Forgive me, it's been a while."

His sarcasm stung, but there he went, deflecting again.

After pulling my dress back up to cover my chest, I turned on my side to face him. "Don't change the subject."

"Jesus Christ," he said, rubbing a hand over his face.

"If, for instance, you had a child, I'd be totally understanding—"

"I don't have a fucking kid," he said, his voice echoing off the bedroom walls. "What the hell do you keep asking me that for? Do you know something that I don't?"

"Hunter, I saw you." It came tumbling out before I could stop it.

He didn't answer right away, only stared at the ceiling, unblinking and weighing his words. "You saw me what, exactly?" His voice was low, like the quiet rumbling of thunder in the distance. The kind that warned of an impending storm. But I'd already said too much now.

"I was worried it was something bad, so when you left yesterday, I followed you and I saw—"

"Wait, stop for a second. You *followed* me?" His head jerked to look at me, his brow raised in disbelief.

"I… Well, I mean, I happened to see—"

"No, you didn't *happen* to see anything. You deliberately followed me. Is that what you're saying?"

"When you say it like that—"

"What did you see?"

"You were at a school and there was this little girl who looked like you—"

"I don't fucking believe this shit," he said, sitting up and yanking his shirt over his head before getting to his feet.

Oh God. I'm an idiot.

"I know, I'm sorry, it's just…you were being so vague about it, and then I got paranoid and—"

Hunter turned around, pinning me with an angry stare. "And what? Did you think I was off dealing meth? Cheating? Skipping out on the job to go to the beach? Please explain to me what the *fuck* you thought I was doing to warrant being followed, Ryleigh."

Shit, he's pissed. I couldn't blame him, but I also needed him to see where I was coming from. "It was stupid, I get that, but when were you going to tell me you have a daughter?"

"That I have a—" He ran his fingers through his hair and gripped the ends as he paced the room. When he stopped, his eyes were wild. "Let's get a few things straight. First, I love that you assume things about me from watching a snippet of my life *out of context*. Second, that you, *you,* of all people would do something like that blows my fucking mind. Did someone put you up to it or was it all your idea?"

I opened my mouth to speak, but he put his hand up.

"You know what, it doesn't even matter," he said. "What I choose to do in my time away from you is *mine*, and if you can't trust me enough to understand that, we have no business being together."

Those words were a hard slap across the face. "I…I do trust you. I just made a mistake. But can't you see that you're at fault here too? How can you say you want me in your life when you're hiding this huge part of you?"

"I'm not hiding anything from you. I have a past, just like you do, and all that heavy shit comes out eventually. *Eventually*, Ryleigh. When I'm ready to talk about it."

He stalked into the kitchen and grabbed his keys from the counter.

"Wait, please don't go," I said, my voice cracking as I blocked him from the front door. "Please don't be mad at me."

"Mad at you?" he scoffed. "The only person I'm mad at is me for thinking I'd finally found someone I wanted to spend time with and get to know. But *this* girl? The one standing in front of me? I don't want to know her. This was a mistake."

My breath caught as he pushed past me, and I grabbed his arm. "What was a mistake? What are you saying?"

"I'm saying this," he said, pointing at me and then back at himself. "You and me. I don't think this is a good idea."

"A good idea," I repeated, wrapping my arms around my waist as if I could hold myself together. My insides felt like Jell-O, like a wobbling mass that could tip over at any moment. "So, what, you want to end things? Break up? Is that what you're saying?"

"I need some space."

"Space like…permanently," I said, not wanting to believe him, but I could see the disbelief and rage still warring in his eyes, in the set of his clenched jaw, in the tension rolling off his body in waves. And the sadness—there was a bit of that too, and that was the part that made my eyes sting with tears. He didn't answer me, didn't have to. His silence said enough.

"I see."

"And that's the thing. No, you don't." He turned his back on me and opened the front door before pausing. Then he looked back over his shoulder as if he wanted to say something else, but then shook his head as if he'd thought better of it.

The door shut, heavy footsteps going down the stairs, and then another door opened and closed. The tears that had threatened to come out finally rolled down my face, and when my legs went unsteady, I reached for the door, resting my forehead on the cool surface.

What just happened? What have I done?

As quickly as our relationship had ignited, the flame had been snuffed out.

Permanently.

I WOKE UP numb the next morning. Actually, I shouldn't say "woke up," considering I didn't get more than a half-hour of sleep all night. My mind was turning, I'd stayed sick to my stomach, and I was seriously considering calling in. To my own business. Which I'd never, ever done.

Instead, I'd trudged to the shower and stayed under the hot water until it ran out. Then I put on black pedal pushers with a green and black polka dot halter and threw my hair up in a messy bun. Yes, messy. *'Cause why not?*

Luckily, I had just planned to work in the kitchen that day, so it wasn't like I had to talk to anyone. Or look toward where I knew Hunter would be all day. I was in the safety zone—at least I was until I covered Amber's lunch break.

"Good afternoon," I said, addressing the young couple that walked in from where I was manning the front register. "Ready to Get Licked?"

Geez, I was really phoning it in today, my words coming out less than enthused. With the contest a week away, I couldn't afford to have my head out of the game, so I plastered a smile on my face and willed it to stay there.

"What can I get for you two today?" I asked.

"Something to share, I think," the woman said, smiling up at the man. His arm was around her, and he gave her a quick squeeze.

"Anything you want," he said.

Oh, gag. Fucking gag me with a spoon already.

"Ooh...what's a Magnum bowl?" she asked, giggling.

"Our specialty Magnum bowls are the largest size you can get, and we currently have four different options. I'm guessing neither of you are here for the Heartbreak Special or the Pity Party for One, so I'd go with either The Diabetes or the Greedy Motherfucker."

"Wow...um." The woman glanced at her partner. "I think the Greedy one sounds better, what do you think?"

"That one works for me."

"Great," I said, not feeling so great at all. "Just let me know which flavor you'd prefer for your handfuls of balls."

They both chuckled, the perfect picture of happily dating bliss. Was this what Hunter and I had looked like? Had people wanted to beat us in the face with an ice cream scooper too? I guess I'd never know.

Once they'd chosen a flavor, I scooped a massive ton of ice cream onto the frozen slab of granite we usually kept in the freezer. Making a large indention in the middle, I began to pile spoonfuls of every topping we offered on top. And I do mean *every* topping. It wasn't called the Greedy Motherfucker for nothing. Then I pulled out what I referred to as "the sledgehammer" and began beating the ingredients into the ice cream to mix them together.

Hmm. Maybe this was the perfect way to release

some of my tension. I could offer a special on this one today to get more people to let me smash stuff. *Good plan.*

The pounding continued as I hammered away, still going even after the ice cream was thoroughly combined.

A hand touched my arm. "I can get it from here," Zoe said. She pushed me back and scooped the battered dessert into a dish bigger than my head and piled it high with whipped cream, nuts, and cherries before sliding it over the counter. "Enjoy," she said, before grabbing my arm and tugging me into the kitchen.

"What are you doing?" she said.

"I was making a Greedy Motherfucker, what did it look like I was doing?"

"Wallowing. Taking your mood out on poor, defenseless piles of goodness. Acting like a crazy person." She threw her hands up in the air. "Take your pick."

"I'm not wallowing."

"You are, and I'm sorry, but you need to take the day off."

My hands went to my hips. "You can't tell me to go home."

"I'm not saying you have to go home, but you can't stay here."

"Not going home," I said, narrowing my eyes.

"Fine. Get in the back booth."

"What? I'm not getting in the back booth."

"Yes, you are. I can't have you on the floor when you're getting this much pleasure out of beating the ice cream to a pulp, and since you hired me to manage your store, I insist. Now go." She pushed me toward the front, and I shuffled away.

"You know, I could fire you," I mumbled, untying my apron and hanging it on the rack.

"You could try," she called out over her shoulder.

Slumping into the only booth that had a black tabletop, I gave a heavy sigh and rested my chin on my palms.

There I was. Relegated to the "Pity Party For One" booth. Not a place I'd ever expected to find myself, but Zoe was right—it was sorely needed today. This was special priority seating, outfitted with headphones should you want to listen to the sad crooning of Adele, a copy of *The Notebook* in paperback, and a box of soft tissues, and a complimentary glass of wine was provided with all orders.

Hey, we have to take care of each other. Looked like it was my turn.

Zoe arrived a few minutes later with one of our four Magnum bowls. This one was what we called The Heartbreak Special, and it was a massive dessert with a serving size that could feed four people. But when you're upset, come on, that's exactly what you need. Ice cream, ice cream, and more ice cream. Oh, and ice cream.

"Don't forget my wine," I said to Z as she walked away.

My spoon sliced into a brownie batter ball, and I shoveled a big chunk in my mouth. *Mmm, this totally helps.*

Well, almost. As long as I could find a way to distract myself from thinking I might've blown something amazing, I'd be okay. The only problem was that I couldn't get the disappointed look in Hunter's eyes out of my mind. Or the way he'd shaken his head in disbelief that I'd snuck around to follow him.

Ugh, I thought around another mouthful. *Stupid stupid stupid.*

But let's get real here. I couldn't completely blame myself. Being burned in prior relationships will have you a little untrusting, sure, but also…would it have been so hard for him to say, hey, there's this kid I pick up a couple times a week, and oh yeah, she's mine. I mean, was that such a big deal?

A nagging feeling in my gut was telling me there was still more he wasn't saying, but I doubted I'd have a chance to ask now. One thing I did know—he wouldn't be coming through that tarp today.

I ate until I got a brain freeze, and when I sat back, I heard a familiar voice. One I definitely wasn't expecting.

"Is there room here for two?" Cameron was looking down at me, dressed in a finely pressed suit, his perfect blond head of hair cocked to the side.

"Hey," I said, and that was all I could manage around a.) being stunned to see him, and b.) having a numb tongue. I motioned to the seat opposite me for him to sit down.

He slid into the booth, unbuttoning his jacket and

looking around the store before his gaze settled on mine. "You hiding back here?"

"Not hiding," I said, poking at the gargantuan scoops still left in my bowl. *How the hell did people eat all this?* I felt like I was drowning in cookie dough, brownies, and fudge, which, let's be honest, is not the worst way to die. I took another bite.

"Then why did Z tell me to come find you at 'The Pit of Despair'?"

"Pity Party for One," I said. "It's just been a rough day. You have those, right? Bad days."

"Any particular reason for that?"

I narrowed my eyes, studying him. "What are you doing here, by the way? Not that I'm not glad to see you, I am, just…well, I haven't seen you since—"

"Since you broke my heart for my best friend?" he teased, and then chuckled. "Nah, I'm just kidding. I was hungry and in the neighborhood, so I thought I'd stop by."

Mhmm, suuuuure. "And that would have nothing to do with someone putting you up to it."

He put his hand over his heart, faking a wounded expression. "That hurts."

I lifted my eyebrows and waited.

"Yeah, I might've heard something went down last night."

"Hah!" I said, wagging my spoon at him. "I knew it."

"But I would've come by anyway. You really do have the best ice cream I've ever had. Not to mention, the owner isn't too bad."

"Dammit. Why do you make me feel like such an asshole?"

"How do I do that?"

"You're just so fucking *nice*."

His lids lowered to half-mast and he said, "I'm not always nice."

"And some lucky girl is gonna reap the benefits of that, trust me." I sighed, shaking my head. "I fucked it all up."

"Did you really follow him?"

I groaned and put my head in my hands.

"I'll take that as a yes," he said. "But I'm sure there's more to the story. My guess is he wasn't exactly forthcoming about where he snuck off to, and that made you suspicious."

"You'd guess right."

"I'd also wager when you confronted him about it, he got defensive and didn't tell you the whole story."

"The whole story? I didn't get a story, period."

He sat back, stroking his broad jaw. "Look, it's not my place to say this, but I know Hunter has feelings for you, and I've seen that guy torture himself enough the past few years. He's been happier the last few weeks than I've ever seen him, and I'm not about to let him throw that away."

I waited patiently for him to continue.

"Back during my first year of college when I met him, he'd just moved here from Chicago and was working in the construction shop on the studio lot where I'd been interning. He was like the older brother I never had, and he really looked out for me while I was still green and paying my dues being the intern bitch."

"I'd like to have seen you be anyone's bitch," I said with a small smile.

He shook his head. "It wasn't pretty. We'd go out, and I was still exploring the whole dating thing after Lauren had gone off with that loser, but Hunter was pretty serious with this one girl. Lily was her name. He'd met her in Chicago while she was still in school, and when she moved back to L.A. to be closer to her family, he followed her. I used to give him such hell for that. And I admit it, I was an asshole. I just wanted to party and meet people and thought he should do the same, but this girl had a kid. A baby, really, by someone she'd met before Hunter."

A baby…before Hunter… The pieces were starting to fit together.

"So what happened?"

"You mind?" he asked, indicating my bowl of melting ice cream. I shook my head and pushed it toward him. "You were putting it to waste. I couldn't help myself." He took a bite and moaned around the spoon. "Seriously, woman, I'm gonna have to hit the gym harder if I come here."

"Oh, please." I tapped my foot impatiently. "So…how long were they together?"

"Something like two years, maybe," he said, licking fudge off his top lip.

"And then they broke up? Was it recently or something?"

He shook his head. "No. Not recently. About"—he thought back—"not quite four years ago now."

"Four years…I don't understand. Why are you telling me all this?"

Cameron pushed the bowl to the side and leaned forward, resting on his forearms. "They were driving home from her brother's place. He'd made a bed or something for Abby, and they were bringing it back. Lily had been begging Hunter to let her drive his new truck, and it had been this kind of running joke since he wouldn't let anyone even touch it. But that day he let her drive…and there was an accident."

"An accident like…like she…" My voice trailed off when the expression on his face remained bleak. *Oh*…not just an accident. The look in his eyes told me she hadn't made it.

I swallowed, my chest tight. "And her baby was—"

"Not with them at the time. Abby, the girl you saw, she was with her grandparents that day." He rubbed his jaw. "Not such a baby anymore, I guess. She'd be six or seven now."

My stomach dropped. No wonder Hunter hadn't said anything. That was a lot to drop on someone you'd known less than a couple months.

"The grandparents have sole custody, and Lily's brother lives about three hours away, so Hunter helps out when he can. Picks her up from school, watches her so they can get a break. She was so young when she lost her mom, but Hunter is familiar to her, and that helped at first."

I kept shaking my head, sadness, sympathy, and shame overwhelming me.

"As you can imagine," Cameron continued, "he wasn't in good shape after. I moved all his stuff into my place so I could at least make sure he ate, and didn't drink himself to death. It took a long time for him to heal, but I don't think he'll ever get over the guilt of what happened, of letting Lily drive, even though it wasn't his fault."

I had no idea what to say. How had he gone through all that, losing the person he loved and being responsible—in his mind, anyway—for it?

"There's a reason I told you all this, and it's also the reason why I let go of you without a fight. Hunter… I mean, I guess women think he's a good-looking guy because he gets approached all the time, but he doesn't really play into all that. I'm not lying when I tell you you're the first woman I've seen him pursue in years."

"Me?" That shocked me like I'd been zapped with a Taser. "Why?"

"You don't see yourself right, do you?" he asked, shaking his head. "You're special, Ryleigh. And hell, so is he under all the cocky bravado he pulls off so well."

"But… But he doesn't want to be with me. He told me that much last night."

"We all say stupid shit when we're mad." Then he

raised an eyebrow. "We also make stupid mistakes and follow people because we're scared of getting hurt."

"So you're saying I should beg him to take me back? That he'd want me to?"

"I think that'd be a good start." He spread his hands wide. "Fix it."

"Easy as that?"

He laughed. "No, I didn't say it'd be easy. He's more stubborn than a horse's ass, so he'll give you a hell of a fight."

"But worth it," I said quietly, tracing the table with my fingertips. "He's worth it." I looked up then. "Thank you for telling me."

"You're welcome. I knew I had to get involved when I saw the doors threatening to come off the hinges."

"He was pretty mad, huh?"

"Yeah, he wasn't in the best mood last night, and that's putting it mildly."

I sighed and dropped my head onto the back of the booth.

Fix it. How was I supposed to do that? I had no idea, but one thing was for sure—I was gonna try like hell.

Chapter Twenty-Two
The After Dark

A FEW DAYS had passed, and I still hadn't spoken to Hunter. Now, before you get all judgy on me that I hadn't moved forward with a plan because I was a chicken shit, I'll have you know the silence *was* part of the plan.

I needed to give him some distance, some time to cool off, and then I'd make my move. It was a genius idea, really, even if it was killing me not to walk the few short steps next door. Lucky for me, we would be purposely running into each other today. Licked…After Dark was finished, and there was a walk-through scheduled for this afternoon, according to Zoe, who'd been acting as messenger.

"You look nervous," Zoe said, glancing at me out of

the corner of her eye as she poured crumbled pralines into a bucket of ice cream to mix together. "Need a paper bag to blow into?"

"Maybe? I think it's more queasiness, so I might have to use the bag for another reason."

"Not in the kitchen, you don't. Now can you please sit down and stop pacing around? You're making *me* nervous."

I took a seat on a stool by the large center island and drummed my hands over the top. I'd stayed away from looking next door, though that had taken an enormous amount of willpower. I'd been dying to get a look, but I hadn't been about to risk running into Hunter until we were both ready.

I glanced up at the clock. Five more minutes until noon, when I'd walk the few feet and see the finished product. Five more minutes until I'd see *him* again and determine whether we could give it another try, or…

Don't think about the or.

"This is ridiculous," I said. "I should be excited, not sweating bullets."

Zoe hummed in agreement. "I was trying not to state the obvious."

"Sometimes I need to hear it."

Four minutes.

Stop watching the damn clock. Looking down at the fitted pinstripe skirt I'd worn that flared below the knee, I wondered if I should go put on something else. Something a little shorter to showcase my legs, since he'd always complimented them and they were pretty covered up right now. Not that I truly thought showing a little leg would change his mind about anything, but I needed all the help I could get.

"I'm gonna go change," I said.

"You don't have time to change. And you don't need to."

"He won't look twice at me in this."

Zoe stopped mixing and ran her eyes over me. Her gaze stopped on the tight fit of my shirt across my chest and she tilted her head. Then her eyes flicked up to mine, and I saw what she saw.

Oh. Oh damn.

"You're good," was all she said before going back to mixing.

I could feel the blush on my cheeks from her perusal. Okay, so I wouldn't change. "Zoe thinks I'm hoooooooott," I singsonged, swinging my legs off the stool.

She shook her head and looked up at the clock. "It's time."

"I still have two minutes left."

Zoe narrowed her eyes, and it had me sliding off the stool and holding my hands up.

"Okay, okay, I'm going." When I got to the end of the kitchen, I glanced back. "Hey, Z? How's my ass in this dress?"

The crumpled bag of caramel whizzed past my head.

"That good? Okay, then."

I scurried out of the room with a smile on my face, but when I got out to the floor, the nerves came back.

Where the tarp had previously been there was now a door that slid into the wall, so I could keep the entry open during business hours of both shops when I wanted to or close it off. Licked was packed today, and I didn't want anyone getting an early glimpse before opening night the following week, so I went outside to enter from the front door.

The heat that welcomed me was like being blast into hell, the sun blinding as I stepped outside. My palms began to sweat, my heart skipping as I stood on the sidewalk staring at the magenta door that stood out in contrast to the black exterior of the After Dark. Both businesses color coordinated, but whereas Licked was open, bright, and inviting with a wall-to-ceiling glass window, the closed-off front of the After Dark suggested a seductive, more intimate experience.

Wiping my hands off on the front of my dress, I steeled myself for what would happen next.

You can do this. It will look amazing. Hunter will be receptive. It'll be okay…more than okay.

With a deep breath, I reached for the handle and stepped inside. It took a moment for my eyes to adjust, and when they did, I was greeted with a view I couldn't have made up in my wildest dreams.

It was stunning. So unbelievably gorgeous that I

stood there, mouth agape, for what had to be minutes as my eyes feasted on what had been transformed from gutted interior into an extraordinary lounge in just a few short weeks.

The ceilings were draped in rich shades of pink and purple fabric that billowed out from the edges of the room, and then pinned to the ceiling in the center. From there, a dramatic chandelier came down, its light reflecting around the darkened space.

And the bar. *Oh my God, the bar.* The top of it moved like hot-pink lava, stretching and swirling into different hues as it traveled up and down the length. Behind it, spotlights shone on the wall, which showcased a massive mural of glamorous poses from Golden Era actresses, all provocatively covered in white sheets. I wanted to cry, so overwhelmed by what I was seeing and that it was *mine*.

Swallowing back that urge, I shook my head and whispered, "Holy shit."

"I'm glad you like it."

The voice from behind had me swiveling to face him. Hunter stood a couple feet away, his hands in his pockets, seemingly casual as he stood there in a black pinstripe button-down and jeans, but the tense set of his shoulders said otherwise. There was a melancholy tilt to his mouth, but still, he looked more handsome than I'd ever seen him. There was nothing I wanted more than to reach for him, to wrap my arms around his neck and breathe him in, but I couldn't do that. Not just yet.

Shaking my head slightly, I said, "No, I don't just like it. I love it."

"Not bad for a few weeks," he said, his eyes trailing along the walls and ceiling behind me.

"Not bad, period."

He inclined his head toward the front. "Come on."

As I followed him, he turned all business, pointing out the work they'd done, describing the detail of what I was seeing. I hadn't noticed when I'd entered, but the fabric that draped along the ceiling also gathered at each corner and trailed down to the floor in an elegant sweep. Each of the booths along the walls were U-shaped with plush padding, and high-top tables were placed sporadically throughout the space. He'd been right about ordering a smaller size to accommodate the walkways, making it easier to get to the bar and back areas. And speaking of the back, we'd forgone the gaming area I'd originally thought about to make a hidden lounge, as well as a series of cozy VIP sections that were as luscious as the rest of the bar.

My vision of the After Dark had been blown out of the fucking water, and by someone who knew what I'd love before even I did. How that was even possible, I had no idea, but as I turned to face him, I felt the damn prick of tears again. But at least this time they were happy ones.

"I don't even know what to say…" I started, but the words wouldn't come.

"You don't have to. I know."

"You do. You know me." My eyes stayed on his,

urging him to read between the lines. *I want you. I need you.*

He looked away from me and nodded at the far wall. "We're still waiting on a couple of the paintings, but those should be in no later than Saturday morning."

"Okay. Thank you."

"You're welcome."

My eyes caught on his shirt again, and when I looked down at my skirt I realized we matched. A small smile crossed my lips, but his gaze wasn't on me to see it.

Try. I have to try…

"Hunter," I said, but he held up a hand.

"Don't. Let's just…leave it alone."

I went still, and then he dropped his hand, giving a heavy sigh.

My heart sank. So he didn't want to hear what I had to say. Didn't want to entertain the thought of there ever being an "us" again.

Clearing his throat, he said, "Once I get the pictures up, I'll drop by with the keys. Sometime before the film crew gets here, I'd imagine." He looked around the space again before his eyes settled back on mine. After a long moment, he said, "Well. I think that's it."

I wasn't ready for him to leave yet, but when his hands went back into his pockets, I heard the jingle of his keys.

No, don't leave. Fuck, just say it…just tell him you want him back. Tell him you were stupid, that you know the truth, and you were wrong not to trust him. Tell him it won't happen again.

Say anything so he won't walk out the door.

The rhythm of my heartbeat counted down from ten, the inevitable coming, but I was powerless to stop it.

…four…three…two…

One.

"I'll see you," he said finally, his eyes piercing mine. Then his back was to me, as he headed toward the door.

Stop him.

"The taping for the show is this Saturday," I called out. He stopped and slowly turned around. "The interview starts at six thirty. I'd… I'd really like it if you could be here. It wouldn't be right if you weren't." I took a small step forward. "Please, Hunter."

His gaze dropped to the floor as he thought it over. Then he looked up, an inscrutable expression on his face. "I'll try to make it if I can."

"Okay," I said softly.

His answer wasn't a no, but it was far from a yes. What was running through his mind right now? Did he want me too and neither of us could manage to spit out the words, or was he eager to get away from me? This wasn't how I'd thought things would go at all.

Pulling the keys out of his pocket, he gave me a long look before nodding. I didn't stop him this time when he left, the bright sunlight spilling into the room briefly as he walked out before vanishing and leaving me alone in the dark again. A metaphor for my time with him if ever there was one.

I'd chickened out. A thousand things I wanted to say, needed to say, but not one of them had come. I'd lost my voice when I'd needed it most. And as I stared at the shut door in front of me, I realized that wasn't the only thing I'd lost.

"CHEERS TO OUR enormously talented friend, who is about to take the world by storm with her naughty shakes. We are so damn proud of you." Quinn held up her glass as Shayne, Paige, and I followed suit.

"To Ryleigh, owner of the best-looking bar in L.A.," Shayne said.

"I didn't see my bed in the back like you promised, but cheers, bitch. You did amazing." Paige blew me an air kiss, and we all clinked glasses before taking sips of the first drinks ever made at the After Dark.

I tried not to feel the guilt at her words *you did amazing,* since I couldn't take credit for any of it. It was all Hunter. And thinking of him and the way he'd left me two days earlier had my heart seizing in my chest, the regret overwhelming.

Forcing him out of my mind, I smiled at my friends, who'd come to help me christen the bar the night before the big show. I could hardly believe that in less than twenty-four hours, I would be done filming and the fate of turning my dream into a reality across the U.S. would be in the hands of thousands of viewers around the country.

For so long I'd thought about what it would be like to have an ice creamery, something I could call my own, something to have complete control of that would reflect everything I was. And now to have *two* incredible businesses… I knew not to take that for granted. And as much as I wished I had the man I wanted to share those dreams with here to celebrate, I had to focus on being grateful. He'd done his part, and now it was time to do mine.

Right? *Right.*

"Thank you, guys. Best friends a girl could have," I said.

"Damn straight," Paige agreed before sucking a cherry between her lips. "So by the way, we've decided to crash your little TV show thing tomorrow. What time should we be here?"

"Really? You'll come?"

Shayne smirked. "You know bloody well we wouldn't miss it."

"And Paige has to make sure she hasn't missed out on screwing any of the hot, eligible men still roaming L.A.," Quinn added.

"Oh come on," Paige said, "you make it sound like all I think about is sex."

All three of us stopped and stared at her.

Paige feigned a hurt expression. "What? I like to

date. Dating and sex don't *always* go hand in hand, ya know."

The three of us looked at each other with raised eyebrows.

"Fuck off, you prudes," Paige said, clinking her glass against each of ours. "And cheers to *that*."

"I know you don't want to hear it, but I have this really great guy at the agency I could set you up with—" Shayne said before Quinn's hand clamped over her mouth.

I shook my head in disapproval. "You know what happens now. Someone revoke her green card. She's threatening us with dates."

"Someone dispatch the INS to remove the alien from the premises," Quinn said.

"I am a *legal* alien, thank you very much, and I have a permanent resident card to prove it." Shayne took her wallet out of her purse and flashed us the card proclaiming what she'd said. "You can't just revoke it for no reason, so kindly go to hell, you arseholes."

Giving a dramatic sigh, I said, "I feel so much love in this room. You think other friends tell each other I love you by flicking them off or telling them to go to hell?"

"If they don't, I feel bad for them," Paige said. "If you can't tell your friends to fuck off with a smile and know they aren't going anywhere, then you don't have real friends."

Quinn flicked her long hair over her shoulder and held up her glass again. "Can we cheers to that? Or over shots this time?"

"Are you trying to get me drunk?" I asked. "I have to be on camera tomorrow, and bags under my eyes don't really go with my outfit."

"Everyone get a glimpse of this lightweight," Paige said, standing up and raising her voice as if addressing a full room. "She gets trashed off a boozy shake and a shot, and she *owns* the bar. You can't trust a non-alcoholic bar owner."

Rolling my eyes, I laughed and slid off my stool. "Exactly why I *am* the owner. Someone has to be sober enough not to confuse the rum with the bourbon in a Pansy Ass."

As I lined up the shot glasses along the gorgeous custom bar top, I looked over at the crazy group of women I called my family. For those few moments in the bar with my friends, the world felt almost right again, and I'd forgotten all about the heaviness in my heart.

Like I said. *Almost.*

Chapter Twenty-Three
Rock the Shit Outta That Shit

THE NEXT DAY I stood outside the entry that joined my two shops, watching the flurry of activity in the After Dark as men set up the lighting and the director went over last-minute checklists with the woman who would be interviewing me. It was beyond surreal, but luckily I had the girls on standby to pinch me whenever I needed it. And I'd needed it several times already.

We'd closed Licked for the day, the first time ever on a Saturday, but I had Zoe and a couple of the other staff on hand for the film crew to get footage of them in action. Zoe, bless her, had colored her hair a bright fuchsia to match the Licked logo, and all of them sported vintage ensembles. I couldn't be prouder.

"Are you nervous yet?" Shayne asked as she sidled up to me and linked her arm through mine. She had her fabulous red curls pinned up on the side with a big white flower and, just like my staff, was wearing a retro sundress in solidarity.

My friends are awesome.

"Terrified," I said. "Why am I doing this again?"

"Because you're depriving everyone outside of L.A. of your genius idea and mouthwatering desserts if you don't share. That would be a crime, and you're not a criminal, so"—she nodded at the cameras—"go kill it."

"Ryleigh? They need you in makeup," Quinn said, as she walked up behind us. Though she was petite, she was a fierce sight in her signature black…well, everything. "Better hurry. Paige is over there getting tips on contouring, and they'll have her looking like a Kardashian soon."

"Oh, good grief." I quickly went over to the tables we had pushed together for hair and makeup to see Paige in a pair of striped shorts and wearing a rocker tee, blazer with rolled-up sleeves, and higher heels than mine. She was trying on a deep shade of lipstick under the approving eye of the makeup artist.

"What do you think?" she asked, looking at us through the mirror. "Too much?"

I eyed the deep wine shade against her blond hair. "Surprisingly, it suits you. I think I'll stick to pink, though."

"You must be Ryleigh." The makeup artist shook my hand. "Let's see what we can do with you today, shall we?"

We went over the color palette, and I showed her my preferences. Although it should've excited me to have someone *else* doing my makeup today, I was more panicked that I'd look nothing like myself when she was done. While she worked, a dark-skinned man in a white suit came over and circled around me, holding his chin in thought. I soon learned he was my hair stylist, and that worried me for a second because the guy was bald. How do you trust a man with *no* hair to do yours? Anyone? Bueller?

"What do you think about a bow?" he asked, his French accent pronounced as he ran his fingers through my tresses.

"A bow? Uh…I haven't put bows in my hair since I was five."

"No, no," he said, holding my hair on top of my head. "Your hair *is* the bow. Your bow is the hair. You see?"

"I don't really know how—"

"Just wait. Trust me, I show you," he said, grabbing a comb and teasing my hair up to high heaven.

Please, God, don't make me look ridiculous today.

I squeezed my eyes shut as they worked, not wanting to see the progress they made until it was all done. But I tried to have a little faith. I mean, French people do great updos, right?

There was a tap on my shoulder what felt like an hour later.

"Miss? Ryleigh? Wake up now and see." The man sounded excited, so I steeled myself for something crazy.

Opening my eyes, the first thing I noticed was the gorgeous shade of pink painted on my lips. *Very nice.* A pair of false eyelashes, long and curled, made my eyes pop, and though I still looked like myself, it was the more glamorous, airbrushed version that would be impossible to maintain in real life. My gaze drifted up to my hair, and it took me a second to realize it *was* my hair. A bow. He'd made it into a freakin' bow sitting on top of my head. It sounded insane when he'd proposed it, but now I was kicking myself for not watching so I could replicate it.

"Wow. This is... Thank you. Could you come by and do this every day? Both of you?" I said.

The Frenchman laughed. "You could not afford me, but merci, chéri."

Mr. Lieberman came over then and went over the final rundown of what would happen. They'd already done the daytime interior and exterior shots, as well as filming my staff in action, so it was almost time for the final part—the interview.

As I greeted my friends with my new look, which they oohed and ahhed over, I casually let my eyes drift over the rest of the shop, looking for the one face I'd been hoping to see but wasn't surprised not to. I knew he'd been by this morning because I'd found the keys he'd left on the bar counter when I went to let the TV crew in. That should've been sign enough, I guess. He hadn't waited to bring them by when he came tonight; instead he'd snuck in and left them without having to see me.

But maybe there was a good reason. He might've left a message…

Ducking into the kitchen, I took my phone out of my purse and scrolled through the "good luck" messages from friends and family, including Cameron. But there was nothing from Hunter. Not a call, not a text—

My phone pinged with a new message alert. I opened it, and, like he'd known I was thinking about him, it was from the man I'd been wishing was here.

Good luck tonight. I know you'll knock 'em dead.

I quickly typed back a "thank you, wish you were here" message and waited, hoping he'd respond and tell me he was on his way or maybe explain why he wasn't coming. But my message never went through, "message delivered" never popping up. Out of curiosity, I called his phone, and it went straight to voicemail, like he'd turned off his cell directly after sending the message.

He wasn't coming. He really *really* wasn't coming. The last bit of hope, the one I'd been clinging to like a lifeline, fell away. Tucking the phone back in my purse, I walked numbly back into Licked, and when my friends caught sight of my face, they ran over.

"He's not coming," I said, and then gave a limp shrug.

"That sonofabitch."

"I will rearrange his arse with his face."

"Give me two minutes with that guy and I'll make him wish he were dead."

I waved my hand as they continued to curse Hunter on my behalf. "Thanks, guys, but it's fine. Really. I'll…you know, hopefully be super busy when I kick this show's ass, right?"

"That's the spirit," Paige said, her arm going around my shoulders. "The poor bastard will be sorry he ever let you go."

No, he's probably doing a happy dance somewhere out there.

"Ryleigh?" Mr. Lieberman called out from the entry. "We're ready for you."

After a group hug, we went over to the After Dark, and I was instructed to sit in one of the two chairs lit up with what looked like spotlights. The girls all gave me thumbs-up signs from where they were seated in director's chairs behind the camera crew, and I took a deep breath.

Don't think about him. Think about the shops you've worked so hard on for the last few years. Think about making your friends and family proud. Don't think about the one who doesn't want to be with you.

As one of the crew members attached a small microphone to my outfit, placing it so it would be out of the camera's view, I let my eyes roam around the space. It was still hard to believe this was mine, and I doubted I'd get used to it anytime soon. There were two new vertical wall hangings on either side of the exit that hadn't been there yesterday. A couple of the final pieces Hunter had come to put up this morning, I guessed. They were of Grace Kelly and Dorothy Dandridge, both fully decked out in glamorous gowns with cocktails in hand—fantastic additions. I'd meant to look for all the last-minute touches earlier today, but the place had been swarming with people on both sides, and I hadn't gotten a chance.

Tony, the lighting director I'd met two weeks prior, stood to my right, fiddling with a light, and I held my hand up to shield my eyes. When he finished his adjustment and moved out of the way, a picture just above the center booth behind him was revealed, and it had the breath rushing out of me.

"Oh my God," I said, unable to tear my gaze away. Standing up, I walked over to the booth, and the closer I got, the more I couldn't believe what I was seeing. The final piece, the one Hunter had waited until today to install, wasn't just any picture, and it definitely wasn't one I'd picked out along with the others. No, this one was personal. An artistic rendering of a photograph taken not long ago, of a couple in happier times, decked out in full fifties flare. The girl was swooped up in her lover's arms, both laughing. Happy. *The Last First Date* was scrawled across the bottom.

My legs were going to give out. I grabbed on to the side of the booth as Quinn dashed over.

"Are you okay? You look like you've seen a—" Quinn stopped and squinted at the picture. "Is that you and—"

"Can you get me my phone?" I said in a breathless rush. "In my purse in the kitchen."

She didn't ask any questions, just ran out of the room and was back in less than thirty seconds. "Here," she said, handing it to me, and with shaky hands, I took it from her.

There were no missed calls, no response from Hunter to the text I'd sent, but it didn't matter as long as he answered the phone now.

But again there was no ringing, just the automated recording as the call went straight to voicemail. I hung up and tried again. Same thing. This time I left a quick message.

"Hunter, it's Ryleigh. Please call me when you get this."

After hanging up, I dialed a different number.

"Hey," Cameron said, answering on the second ring. "Aren't you supposed to be—"

"Sorry, but is Hunter with you? It's urgent."

A hand touched my elbow, and I whipped around. I must've had a crazy expression on my face, because the assistant backed up.

"Sorry, but they're calling for places now," she said, her thumb pointing back at the chairs where the host was already seated and getting miked.

"Cameron, hang on." Covering the phone with my hand, I said, "I'm so sorry, can I just have a second, please? It's an emergency." Then I turned and put the cell back to my ear. "Hello? You there?"

"Yeah, I'm here, but no, he's not with me. Is

everything okay? I thought you were filming."

"I am, but I..." How was I going to explain that I knew what the picture meant? It wasn't over. He'd never have put that up if there wasn't hope of another chance. "I just need to find him. Please."

"Ryleigh..." he said. "I don't know how to tell you this, but he's gone."

That one four-letter word had me leaning against the booth for support. Gone? What did he mean *gone*? "Well...where did he go? He was just here this morning."

"He left for the airport a few minutes ago. Back to Chicago."

"What?" I shouted. I could feel the weight of everyone's stares on me as they turned in my direction, but in that moment, I couldn't care less.

"I'm sorry," Cameron said. "I thought you knew."

"No...no, no, no, no, no. Why would he do that? He left the picture, that means..." Well, fuck. I thought it meant... Well, maybe it didn't mean... Oh God, even my thoughts weren't making any sense.

"Ryleigh, we need to get started." Mr. Lieberman was at my side, a stern expression on his face as he checked his watch.

"Right. I'm coming." As he ushered me back to my chair, I asked Cameron, "Burbank airport?"

"LAX," was all I heard before Quinn was in front of me.

"I need to take this," she whispered, and I let the

phone go without a fight.

"He's leaving," I said, my voice barely audible.

"Hunter?" Her brows knitted together. "Where?"

"LAX..." I shook my head as I passed, walking in a daze back to the set.

"All right, there she is. Are you ready?" one of the co-anchors of *Wake up America,* Sheila, asked in a perky voice as I sat down. "Oh, don't be scared, I promise to go easy on you."

He's leaving. He's leaving me. *Permanently?*

Mr. Lieberman's voice rang out: "Can we get someone in makeup? She's looking a little pale."

The makeup artist was there in a flash, touching up my face and lips.

If he just left for LAX, I could be there before him...

A clapperboard went off, followed by the word "Action," and it jolted me back to reality.

Sheila gave me a pleasant smile and said, "Ryleigh Phillips. As the owner of Licked, an eccentric ice creamery in West Hollywood that specializes in delectable desserts with flavors not suitable for children, you must get asked often where the inspiration for your shop came from. Could you tell us a little background?"

But even if I went to LAX...what airline? What time is his flight?

I swallowed, my throat constricting and blocking off my air supply. Beads of sweat formed on my brow, and all I could focus on were how bright and hot the lights were, and that Sheila still had a smudge of lipstick on her front teeth.

"Uh…" *Breathe and answer the question. Wait, what was the question? Names…uh…desserts? Inspiration?* Trying for a smile, I said, "The uh…inspiration comes from…um." My gaze wandered toward the camera, and I could see the faces of my friends staring at me with encouraging expressions. "I'm sorry, can you repeat the question, please?" I asked.

Quinn still had my phone in her hand, and my eyes were glued to it while Sheila repeated the question. Which I missed. Again.

It was hot, so damn hot, and I wiped above my upper lip with the back of my hand.

"Cut," the director shouted, and then Ms. Watts added, "I can see the sweat dripping down her face, so can we please get someone with a mop and bucket sometime this century?"

The makeup artist quickly ran over to powder me in an effort to keep the thick layers of paint from sliding off, but I had a feeling there was no amount of makeup that could help in my current state. "Just calm down a bit, sweetie, and it'll stay on better," she said, and then lifted my chin to make sure she got it all before heading back to the sidelines.

Calm down… How could I calm down? My nerves were shot, and as much as I tried to keep my focus on how amazing this opportunity was, my mind kept drifting to Hunter. He was getting on a plane, and once he did that, I'd lose him. *I can't lose him. Not without telling him how much he means to me.*

He'd been the one to pursue me, and now it was my turn. I hadn't fought hard enough… Hell, I hadn't fought at all. The one time I'd had a chance to make him listen and I'd frozen.

What if this is my only chance?

And that was when I knew. There wasn't even a choice.

Holding up my hand to shield the light, I squinted, searching out Quinn. When I found her, the look on her face was one of sympathy.

"Quinn…" I couldn't get the words out, but somehow she understood.

Nodding, she mouthed, *On it,* and pulled out her keys from her jeans pocket, whispering to Paige before running out the door and hauling Shayne with her. Then Paige headed straight for me.

"I'm so sorry," she said to the producers as she took my arm and helped me to my feet. "But there's been a family emergency, and we have to leave."

"Leave?" Ms. Watts repeated, scoffing from where she'd been sitting and picking at her long, manicured nails. "You can't just leave. We're in the middle of a shoot."

"We apologize for the inconvenience," she said as she wrapped her arm around my waist and walked us to the exit. "Thank you for the opportunity."

As she pushed the door open, Ms. Watts called out, "You leave and none of this airs—" Then the door shut, cutting off her threats.

Quinn's black sports car was already at the curb, and Paige pushed me inside the backseat before rounding the trunk and getting in on the other side.

"Let's go," she said, and the car squealed as Quinn hit the gas.

Chapter Twenty-Four

Gone in Sixty Seconds

I TOOK DEEP breaths, and as my body temperature cooled off under the heavy air conditioning, the realization that I'd just walked out of the show taping to chase after Hunter hit me. It was as if under the lights my brain had melted like ice cream left in the sun and was now solidifying back together. "Oh fuck me," I said. "Did I just… Did we leave the taping? Did that just happen?"

"Yep, and en route to rescue your man so you can make your big declaration of love," Quinn confirmed.

A jackhammering began in my chest. "But…we don't even know which airline or what time or anything. He could already be gone. Oh shit. Shit shit."

Shayne turned around in the passenger seat and held

up my phone. "Actually, Cameron just filled me in, and he said Hunter is on the nine o'clock American Airlines flight to Chicago. We should catch him just in time." She eyed the dashboard and raised an eyebrow at the forty-five miles per hour Quinn was currently doing. "Maybe."

"This is crazy," I said, and began to laugh deliriously. I was losing my mind. "Who does this in real life?"

"You do, and we're helping. Quinn, can you maybe push on the gas up there?" Paige said, as she dumped the contents of her makeup bag in her lap and rummaged through until she found what she was looking for. Then she twisted toward me and blotted under my eyes with a sponge. "I thought you were gonna pass out up there. Your face was literally sliding off."

As she touched up my skin, I began to panic. "I just left all those people in my shop… I forgot my purse…"

"I got your purse on the way out, and I'm talking to Zoe now. She's going back to close things down," Shayne said, the phone pressed to her ear.

"That's better," Paige said, as she looked over her handiwork. "Now start thinking about your speech."

"My speech?"

"Yes, the lovey-dovey romantic speech that's gonna convince him to stay. Let's hear it."

Swallowing thickly, I thought back to the reason I'd made such a rash decision in the first place. The picture. The one of the two of us in front of the Hollywood Bowl marquee on our first date. It was the final, missing piece of the After Dark, and so was the man in the photo who had stolen my heart.

"Don't you dare get on the 10. We'll never get there in time," Paige told Quinn. I usually hated when she became a backseat driver and dictated directions, but at that moment, I was grateful. I just needed to get there faster.

Paige leaned forward between the front two seats. "No, no, no, it'll take us to the 405 and it's a fucking gridlock. It's quicker just to go Fairfax to La Cienega.

"I know the way to the airport, Paige, don't make me pull over," Quinn said.

"I wouldn't have to tell you how to get there if you didn't drive like my granny."

Quinn's eyes narrowed in the rearview mirror. "Hey, Paige?"

"Yeah?"

"Fuck off." With that, Quinn swerved into the left lane, switching gears and slamming her foot on the accelerator.

Paige whooped in the backseat and jumped up and down as Shayne and I both grabbed the handles above our heads and held on for dear life. Quinn drove with the speed of a racecar driver, and, surprisingly, just as smooth—not that it made me any less apprehensive about running headfirst into a tree.

"Where the hell did you learn how to drive like this?" Paige asked. "You've been holding out on us. Damn government agent."

Quinn stuck a choice finger in the air and then jerked the car back to the right lane, passing a trio of slower cars taking up the fast lane. "Move it or lose it," she called out as we sped by.

But as we neared the airport terminal drop-off, we hit a wall of traffic. A big wall.

"Oh no," Shayne said. "Do you think you could make a run for it in your heels from here?"

"Fuck no, she's not running for it," Quinn said, and then wrenched the car half onto the sidewalk to bypass the long line. When she couldn't go any farther, she began laying on the horn and rolled down Paige's window. "Do your magic, woman."

Paige stuck her body halfway out the window, directing the cars to move or stop, but it was when she flashed one carful of guys that they immediately veered off to the side to let us in front of them. When she pulled herself back into the car and rolled up her window, I laughed. "I appreciate that you just flashed half the city to get me there faster."

"Oh, please," Quinn said, and I caught her shaking her head in the mirror. "You know she likes to show them off whenever she gets a chance. We just did *her* a favor."

With the worst of the traffic behind us, it only took a few minutes to get to the drop-off for Terminal 4. When we finally pulled up to the curb, I jumped out amid their catcalls and shouts of encouragement, and then they went off in search of parking.

Here we go.

I sprinted inside, my eyes searching for the man who would *not* be getting on that plane today. Of course he'd chosen the airline with the biggest presence at LAX. There were more than a handful of counters, and they were packed with passengers. My anxiety mounted as I realized that I could've come this far and might still miss him. After searching the line at the first counter, I dashed off to the second. He wasn't there either, and with the time of his flight drawing nearer every second, my chances of finding him were running out like sand through an hourglass.

No sign of Hunter in the third line either, and as I turned to run to the next one, I hit a brick wall. Well, not literally a brick wall, but it sure as hell felt like it.

"Can I help you, ma'am?" The security guard I'd smacked into was looking down at me with suspicion, an eyebrow cocked, his voice gruff and no-nonsense. "Do you have a boarding pass?"

"Uh, no," I said, breathless. "I don't, I'm just looking for someone." My eyes continued to search around the guard. *Please be here. Please let me find you.*

"Ma'am, I'm going to have to ask you to leave if you're not boarding a flight today."

"But I have to find him," I said. "He can't get on the plane, and I have to tell him that. Can you please just…help me or something?"

"Is there a reason you're adamant he not board the

plane?"

Shit, I knew what he was thinking. "It's nothing to do with the plane, he just can't leave, so please—"

"Ma'am, you're not boarding today, so I'm afraid I'll have to escort you off the premises."

"No, look, I'll buy a ticket, okay, I just have to—" I lost my train of thought as the crowd parted and Hunter's face came into view. He was at one of the automated stations a hundred feet away, hefting a bag back up his shoulder before taking his ticket from the dispenser.

"He's here," I said to myself, and then looked up at the guard. "That guy right there. Let me just... Please just let me talk to him and then I'll leave. I promise." My eyes darted back to Hunter, where he was walking toward the baggage drop with a large suitcase. "Look, you can even come with me, okay?" I held up my hands in submission as I moved around him, and when it was clear he would follow me, I turned around toward the direction Hunter had last been. Wait...he wasn't there anymore. I scanned the crowd and saw the back of him as he headed for the escalator.

"Hunter!" I called out, and when he didn't turn, I jogged his way—yes, *jogged* in my heels—and yelled his name again. This time he heard me, and he looked around, his brows knitted together. When he saw me, his eyes widened and he turned back to face me.

The adrenaline and physical exertion had me out of breath when I caught up to him, my security escort hot on my trail.

"Ryleigh," he said, looking between me and the guard in confusion. "What's going on?"

"I had to…catch you," I said, panting, my hands on my hips as I tried to catch my breath. "Just…a sec." When I could breathe again, I cleared my throat. "I made a mistake. A horrible mistake."

"What are you talking about? How did you even know I was here?"

"It doesn't matter. What matters is that you can't get on that plane. I won't let you."

His eyebrows shot up, the tiniest curve to his lips. "Won't let me," he repeated. "And I suppose this gentleman with you is the force behind that statement."

"Uh, no. Actually, I'm pretty sure he's going to arrest me after this. But I couldn't let you leave without telling you everything I wanted to say but was too scared to *actually* say when I had the chance, so here goes."

I took a deep breath and smoothed my hands down my skirt before looking him in the eye. And suddenly, I didn't feel nervous anymore. I knew those eyes. I knew every line of his face, the way he felt under my hands, and the way he tasted on my lips. The way he looked at me was the way no one had ever looked at me in my life. People always say when you know, you know, and though I'd never understood how that could possibly be true, it all made sense now. Nothing would ever be as right as it was with the man in front of me by my side, and that knowledge was all the courage I needed to speak freely.

I paused to take another deep breath. "The first thing I owe you is an apology. I made a *huge* lapse in judgment thinking it was no big deal to follow you. It was wrong, I knew better, and I hurt you. But I'm sorry. I'm not perfect, and I made a mistake. I didn't mean to break your trust, and I can only promise I won't do it again. I was just..." As he watched me with those penetrating eyes, I dropped my shoulders and gave him a sad smile. "I guess I was just desperate to know you."

"Ryleigh—" he said.

"That's not an excuse, I know. I'm not making one. It's just...well, I saw the picture you put up and I thought that meant maybe you..."

Maybe you wanted to be with me.

"Maybe I what?" he asked, letting go of his carry-on and crossing his arms over his chest. When my eyes took in the defensive posture, I panicked, feeling an irrational surge of anger at him for just leaving without so much as a goodbye.

"Look," I said, "you can't just leave that picture of us up in my bar and expect to sneak off to Chicago and forget about me while I have to look at it every single day. How is that fair? It's not, so fuck you for that."

A cough came from behind me and I looked over my shoulder to see the security guard shaking his head. "If this is your idea of stopping him from getting on that plane, lady, you might want to rethink it."

"Thank you, I wasn't done yet," I said, facing Hunter

again. There was a sparkle of amusement in his eyes as he waited patiently for me to continue.

"And you have your business here, you have…you know, you have Abby. You can't leave Cameron, he would probably forget to feed the fish in the coffee table, so you could get charged with homicide."

Hunter's lips twisted. "So you're telling me I should stay to save the fish?"

"No. Well, yes. I mean, fish are important too, but… Fuck, sorry, I know none of this is coming out right." *Come on, Ryleigh, get it out.* "The thing is—"

The loudspeaker came on, drowning out my words, so I waited until it was finished to speak again.

"From the moment I met you, I haven't been able to take my eyes off you. And I wanted to, trust me, I wanted to. I thought you were this arrogant guy who could date any woman he wanted to and probably did. And I had been so caught up in looking in the wrong direction that I failed to see you at first. Really see you, the way you saw me. The way I hope you still do. Still will."

"Ryleigh—"

"No, let me finish. I want you. Here. With me. To give us another shot, because I really think we've got something amazing. More than amazing…life-changing. When I looked around the After Dark today, all I could think was that this has all been beyond anything I thought was possible. You made my dream come true, and I'm not sure I could ever thank you enough for that." As he opened his mouth to respond, I held up my hand. "But my dream wasn't just the After Dark. Or Licked. Or the show. My biggest dream was you."

His mouth parted as I continued.

"So you see, you can't get on that plane. This can't be the end."

"Ryleigh…" he said finally, and then stopped as the announcer came over the loudspeaker again, rattling off boarding cutoff times. "Shit." His eyes were full of regret as they met mine. "Ryleigh…that's my flight."

Chapter Twenty-Five

Last Dance

"DON'T GET ON the plane," I said, taking a step toward him. "Please. Just…think about it. Think about us."

He looked down at the ground, his hand running through his hair. I didn't breathe while I waited. At least not until a family of four shoved by, their suitcases knocking into me as they rushed past. They were probably running to the same gate he should've been running to. Watching them go, I half joked, "Okay, you might have to think a little faster."

He looked up at me then, one side of his mouth tipped up in the smallest hint of a smile. Then it fell.

"What about the show?" he asked.

Oh, right. The show. The one I'd walked out on. That

was gonna be a disaster. "I'm sure they got what they needed and we'll see how it goes."

Shaking his head slowly, he said, "I can't believe you came all the way down here for me."

Thump…thump. My heart was pounding, and I could only nod.

"You're fucking crazy, you know that?" he said.

"Sometimes."

The final call for his flight sounded over the intercom, and the security guard stepped up next to me.

"If that's your flight, you're about to miss it," he said to Hunter.

Thump…thump…thump…

Hunter let out a heavy sigh and stepped forward to cup my face in his hands.

Yes…yes, he was going to kiss me and then we'd make up for all the lost time…

I closed my eyes and tilted my head up as his face drew closer, and then I felt the warmth of his lips against my forehead.

"I'm sorry," he said, against my skin. Then he kissed my head, but not in the way you would with a lover. It was too platonic, too much like a goodbye kiss. When he pulled away, he whispered, "I have to go."

As he backed away, my fingers lost their hold on his shirt, and then he grabbed the handle of his carry-on and headed straight for the escalator without looking back.

He's leaving. He's really leaving. And there's not a thing I can do.

I felt numb as I watched him, like it wasn't really happening and he'd turn back and tell me he was joking any minute.

Had I been that horrible? Had it been too much to overcome? I didn't believe that, and I didn't believe he was walking away. But there he was, slipping further out of my grasp. As he reached the top of the escalator, he looked briefly over his shoulder, his eyes landing on mine, and I wished I could say there was regret there, but he was too far away.

It was over.

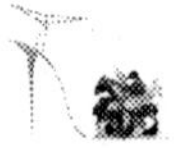

THE STREETLIGHT FLICKERED above, nightfall already a dark blanket across the sky as I climbed out of Quinn's car. The drive back home had been a silent one. There had been no need for more words, but Paige had kept a firm grip on my hand, the only show of support I could handle right now.

Knowing I needed to be alone, they'd let me out without a fight, without following me around and making sure I was okay. That's what the people do who truly know and love you—give you space when you need it.

I took out my keys, unlocked the door that led to Licked, and went inside. There was no trace of anyone having been there; the tables and chairs were back in order, the lights turned off.

It was quiet, so quiet.

Walking over to the jukebox, I flipped through the songs until I found the ones I wanted and then pressed the buttons to keep a steady stream going.

As the sounds of Ella Fitzgerald filled the space, I crossed through to the After Dark. It, too, was back to normal. For what had taken hours to set up, the lights and cameras had been packed up and moved out quickly. I flipped on the switch for the bar, the pink lighting up and casting a glow around the room. Mindlessly running my hand down the length of the bar top, I let my eyes roam around the small details and touches Hunter had put into every inch of the space. Would I ever be able to come in here and not think of him? Would I want to?

Sighing, I let my hand drop and sang along softly to the song playing as I crossed over to the picture I didn't need to look at, but I couldn't help it. It hadn't meant a thing to him. It was just another picture, just another piece of his job. But it had meant something to me. And even if he wasn't mine any longer, he *was* the reason I had this beautiful space to call my own.

The jingle of the front door to Licked alerted me to someone entering the shop.

"We're closed," I called out, belatedly remembering I didn't lock the door when I'd come inside.

A figure in the shadows stepped toward the entry to

the After Dark, and as his body filled the doorway, I didn't need to see his face to feel who he was.

"That's too bad," Hunter said, coming into the room. "I was hoping you still had your Jackass Special available."

The burn of tears blurred my vision as my heart caught in my throat. *How is he… What is he… Is he really here?*

"Sorry," I said when I could speak. "All sold out of Jackass today."

He circled around to my left and I pivoted my body to face him. "What about… What's the one you recommended? Wanker, was it?"

"Out of those too."

"Maybe I'll just try an On My Knees and Begging Forgiveness Sundae today."

As a tear escaped, I wiped my face with the back of my hand. "I'm not familiar with that one."

"No? See, first you start off with a scoop of I Don't Know What The Fuck I Was Thinking. Then you pile on the Really Stupid Decisions, and you end with some pretty epic Begging scoops."

"Sounds like one of the Magnum bowls," I said, cracking a smile before letting it fall. "What are you doing here, Hunter?"

"I couldn't let you get the last word." He stopped and turned his ear toward the jukebox. "Do you always listen to sad songs in the dark?"

I shook my head slowly. "No. And this isn't a sad song. It's about hope."

"Really," he said, facing me again. "She sounds sad."

"Can't you be both?"

He blew out a breath, his hand in his hair. "Ryleigh... It's been...a really long time since I've been here. Opening up to someone, showing them who I am. Which is crazy, because that's what attracted me to you. You are who you are. You don't wear your baggage. You own it. Completely. I can't say the same for me, and I know I've fucked this up badly. I should never have left that night without us getting everything out in the open, and I should've crawled back to you every day since. I didn't know how to deal with my past. How to explain about Abby without telling you all that heavy shit that I just wasn't ready for you to have to handle too."

He took a step closer, his eyes on mine. "But that was selfish. Because if there's anything you've taught me, it's that when you love someone, you love all of them, and not just the parts they want you to see. You have to embrace the ugly parts. The parts that are hard, that are scared. The ones that are awkward and don't fit in."

Stopping in front of me, he said, "I'm sorry," and I could feel the truth of his words in my bones. "I'm so sorry. It scares me to want you as much as I do, because you could hurt me. Break me. And I've been broken before." He stopped and rubbed his forehead. "But that's not a good enough reason to stay away from you. And I don't want to."

I swallowed hard, unable to speak, but memorizing everything he said. He wanted to be with me. He was scared. He was sorry.

"Please tell me I'm not too late—" he said, but before he could get the words completely out, I threw my arms around his neck. Caught off guard, he hesitated for only a second before wrapping me in his strong embrace.

The feel of him against me had my body sighing, filling a hole in me that had been left gaping in his absence.

"I missed you," I said, my voice muffled against his neck.

His arms tightened around me. "You won't have to miss me again. I promise."

He held me as the sounds of Ella washed over us, and gently, ever so gently, we began to sway with the music.

"I didn't realize you were a dancer," I said, leaning back to look at him. He reached up and wiped the rest of the tears from my face.

"Hopefully I'll have more good surprises up my sleeve for you to find."

A smile spread across my face. "I do love good surprises."

His lips found mine, soft at first, but growing in intensity, taking my breath away. I loved the way his tongue moved against mine, perfectly in sync. Loved the taste of him and the way he held the back of my neck so firm, like I was his most cherished possession.

As the song ended and the next one started, he pulled away.

"Ryleigh," he said, his voice serious. "There's

something I didn't get the chance to tell you before."

My stomach dropped as I waited for the ball to drop.

He cupped my face, his thumb stroking my cheek. "I really, really love..."

My heart jumped. *Love?*

I held my breath as I waited for his next words.

"Your hair," he said.

My...

I pulled out of his grasp. "What?"

"This bow," he said, fingering the stiff loops on top of my head. "I can't stop staring at it."

My jaw dropped. "You really love my *bow*? That's what you really love?"

"Well, it's a great bow," he said, and then a huge grin took over his face when he caught my expression, unable to hold back his laughter anymore.

"You know, maybe I *do* have some Jackass Specials left. Let me go check." But as I brushed by him, he grabbed my arm, pulling me to his body. His arms went around me again, holding me close, my back to his stomach.

"Can I ask you a question?" I said.

"Anything."

I turned to face him. "Why were you moving back to Chicago?"

"Moving back? I was just going to help my dad with a job for a week."

"What?"

"You thought I was moving back?"

"Well, yeah," I said. When he started laughing, I pushed against his chest. "That's not funny. I panicked. I heard LAX and Chicago, and my brain just went there. But do you mean to tell me I just chased you across town, risked jail time, and had my friends flashing everyone when you were only leaving for one measly week?"

He whistled. "I'm gonna have to do something big to make it up to you."

"Promises, promises."

"I think the first thing will be making sure your TV special airs, since I'm the reason you skipped out on it."

"Wait. How'd you know I ran out?"

"I got an earful from Cameron on the way over here."

I threw my hands up. "*Now* you answer the phone."

He smiled, a sexy-as-hell smile that had me reaching up to kiss it off his face.

"Ryleigh?" he said against my lips.

"Yes?"

He drew his head back to look me in the eye. "I love you. I love your originality. I love the way you fight for what you want. I love the way you never back down from who you are. I love the insane ice cream names that come out of your warped mind and the fact that you make them so fucking good people become addicted. Like me." His smile then could've melted glaciers. "And all those things I don't know about you yet—I love those too."

Smiling through my happy tears, I said, "That's a lot

of love, mister."

"You don't deserve anything less." He brought my face to his, and as the sweet taste of his breath hit my lips, he said, "And Ry?"

"Hmm?"

"I'm keeping you."

The End

Hooker

Book Two of the L.A. Liaisons Series

Available Now!

Thank you for reading Licked. I hope you enjoyed my sassy girls!

* Reviews are vital in spreading the word about our books. If you enjoyed Licked, please consider leaving a review. I'll make sure Ryleigh sends you a Spank You, Sexy Bitch boozy shake.

* For all access to my latest book news + exclusive excerpts, teasers, and giveaways, make sure to join my newsletter at www.BrookeBlaine.com!

Ella - There is no way this book would be in existence without you. Not only do you keep me sane (okay, as sane as possible for me lol), and serve as the best critique partner evahhhh, but you seriously outdid yourself with the gorgeous formatting and the amazing book trailer for Licked. To say you're talented beyond what is fair would be an understatement, and your generosity knows no bounds. I lucked the hell out when you found me, and if there's one thing GR did right, it was pairing the two of us together. Thank you, thank you, thank you for every little thing you do for me… I couldn't possibly tell you that enough. Even without all the work stuff it's more than enough just to have you in my corner. Love you times infinity. Nope. More than that. Oh, and another thing—I'm sorry for the ice cream diet I put us both on for months during the course of writing this book. I promise I'll calm it down for book two and buy us gym memberships. Maybe.

To the Admins of The Naughty Umbrella: Jen, Donna, & Stacy – What a fab trio you hookers are! Thank you for always having my back, for the daily laughs, the necessary venting, and just for being a huge part of my life. I always appreciate your eyes on my stories before they go out into the world, so spank you for that as well. I love your faces offffffff.

Thank you to Judy, Renee K, & Bianca for making this book squeaky clean! Freakin' eagle eyes, all of you! I'm super grateful to work with you and have your support and friendship. Muah!

Massive love to my cover designer, Hang Le. Woman! You did a phenomenal job designing Licked, and I know I've told you that a million times already. You always "get" what I'm going for, and I'm so thankful I can let go of a bit of control (Who, me? Controlling? Pshh.) knowing my covers are safe in your hands. Thank you and tackle hugs!

Most people dread edits, but I actually look forward to mine. That's crazy, right? A huge thank you to my endlessly entertaining editor, Arran McNicol, who makes my shit...err, not shit anymore.

To Chas and Rockstar PR & Literary Agency who handled the cover reveal and blog tour/promo for Licked—I can't thank you enough for taking that huge weight off my shoulders. I appreciate you going above and beyond for me, and I'm so happy to have worked with you on my little bookie book.

Special thanks to Kari March Designs for the sweeeeet teasers! Love them so much. And Heather gets a big thank you for sending me your way too!

Once again, I must thank *and* apologize to my neglected family and friends. I miss birthdays, get togethers, weddings, and all kinds of super fun stuff, but I'm so grateful you understand why and know it won't be forever. Thank you for that. Crystal, Mom, Meme, Ann, and way too many to name. You know I love you, right? Bahamas vacation coming. Really.

Licked is based in Los Angeles because that city opened its arms and gave me a helluva welcome when I moved across country all by my lonesome several years ago. I'm grateful I could call it home for a while, and I wanted a way to show my deep affection for such a beautiful, diverse city. Not only that, I wanted this series to reflect how amazing female friendships can be, and that when you're far from loved ones, you really do make your friends your family. I'm grateful for the bonds I made with several outstanding women while I was there, so Sabrina, Jemma, Eliza, Erin, Julie D, & Kelli—I miss you every day, but no matter where we are, we're never really that far. Hell, that goes for ALL of my friends. Love you bitches.

Speaking of fab women…I can't forget my Brella's! To everyone who makes up our amazing little group, The

Naughty Umbrella—thank you for providing such a fun, positive, supportive safe haven for Ella and me to share ourselves and also have the opportunity to get to know each and every one of you. I hope I get to meet every damn one of you in the near future. Prepare yourselves for some craaaaaazy bear hugs!

A great big mega huge thank you to the bloggers who've written reviews and helped spread the word about my novels. You make it possible for my books to be seen, and I don't take your support lightly.

To YOU (yes, YOU, kickass reader!) for picking up Licked when you probably have hundreds of other novels on your reading devices that are just waiting to be read. There's no way to tell you how much I appreciate you, but if you shoot me an email or find me on social media, I'd like to try.

xoxox

~Brooke

About the Author

About Brooke

You could say Brooke Blaine was a book-a-holic from the time she knew how to read; she used to tell her mother that curling up with one at 4 a.m. before elementary school was her 'quiet time.' Not much has changed except for the espresso I.V. pump she now carries around and the size of her onesie pajamas.

Brooke enjoys writing sassy contemporary romance, whether in the form of comedy, suspense, or erotica. The latter has scarred her conservative Southern family for life, bless their hearts.

If you'd like to get in touch with Brooke, she's easy to find - just keep an ear out for the Rick Astley ringtone that's dominated her cell phone for ten years.